THE WEDDING WEEKEND

RAIN CITY TALES BOOK FOUR

BRENT ARCHER

For Greg, Elle, Delilah, and Maia
with love and gratitude.

ACKNOWLEDGEMENTS

Thanks to Delilah Devlin and Elle James
for the advice and support!

Author's Note

Check out Brent Archer's other stories:

For other works by Brent Archer and release dates on
upcoming new stories, visit
www.brentarcher.net

Follow Brent on Twitter, Like him on Facebook, and
come visit his Instagram page.
twitter.com/brentarcherwrit
facebook.com/brent.archer.186
instagram.com/brent_archer_writer

CHAPTER ONE

C LARK ADAMSON'S FINGERS trembled as he clicked
SUBMIT. Three weeks until his sister Grace's
wedding, and he didn't have a date. He'd grown tired of
the whole gay dating scene in Seattle. Several dinners had
been ruined by judgmental and bitchy guys, and he'd
finally given up finding anyone in the various bars and
clubs.

Still, the red-circled date on the calendar above his
open laptop screamed *loser* unless he found someone to go
with him. When his best friend, Roger Matthews, bowed
out, he turned to his only remaining solution.

He searched the escort ads. Men of every flavor popu-
lated the "men-for-men" sites, advertising all sorts of
services from mild to wild.

Contemplating what "wild" might entail, he rejected
several of the escorts right away. Three pages of ads later,
he narrowed down the choices to a handsome Asian guy,
who enjoyed fine dining and offered a "boyfriend"
experience; a dark-haired, exotic-looking Pacific Islander
with some interesting tattoos, advertising a commanding
knowledge of current events; and a blond twink who
seemed quite sweet, judging from the description of his

interests and services.

Clark flipped to one more site and stopped at the first ad. *Whoa.* Mitch Hampton. Six-foot-four, red hair, blue eyes, and washboard abs. He scanned the ad:

Hey Guys, thanks for checking me out. I provide a relaxing connection, completely focusing on your needs. Boyfriend experience, long weekends, and romantic dinners are my specialty. College-educated and intellectually curious, I can converse on many diverse topics. Other services, more toward mild than wild. Regularly tested and completely bug and disease free. Selective about my client base, so rest assured you are safe in my hands and my bed. Looking forward to hearing from you soon. Contact details below.

After sending a quick message, Clark scrolled through the pictures of Mitch's hairless chest, the tattoo of a toucan on his shoulder, and his long-muscled legs. In the last photo on the profile, the escort posed looking over his shoulder with a grin on his face, gaze fixed on the photographer, with his tapered waist and pert ass on full display.

Clark's ringing cell interrupted his gawking. Glancing at the unfamiliar number, he frowned but accepted the call. "Hello?"

A deep, sexy voice answered him. "Hi, is this Clark?"

"Yes," Clark replied warily. The last thing he wanted was some telemarketer or survey.

"Mitch Hampton, here. You sent me an e-mail asking about my services."

Clark's mouth slackened, and his stomach quivered. He nearly dropped the phone. "Oh, yes, hi," he croaked then cleared his throat. "Thanks for getting back to me so fast."

"I was on my email when your message came through," he replied in a pleasant yet sultry tone. "What can I do for you?"

"Um, well. Here's the deal. My sister is getting married in three weeks." He paused, not wanting to sound desperate. With a sigh, he screwed up his courage. "I need a date."

"That's cool. When is the stressful occasion?"

Chuckling, Clark glanced at the calendar, his nerves settling somewhat. "The wedding is on the twenty-fifth, but I'd need you the afternoon of the twenty-fourth through the afternoon of the twenty-sixth."

After a moment's pause, Mitch continued. "I'm available that weekend. Do you want to connect before you make the final decision? We'd have a chance to see if we're compatible."

The thought hadn't occurred to actually *meet* the escort before the wedding weekend. The phrase from Mitch's ad came to his mind: *Selective about my client base.* The concern about compatibility gave Clark some confidence that hiring Mitch was the right decision. "Maybe. Would you charge me for that?"

Mitch laughed. "Yeah, but I'd give you a discount on the weekend if we click and you want to book with me after the meeting."

Clark frowned again. "How much?"

"One hundred to chat for an hour. Two hundred fifty if you want to do more than talk. If you book, the weekend is four grand, and you cover expenses, though I'll help out with drinks and meals. I have a tux suitable for a wedding, so no need to rent one for me." The escort paused. "Will the ceremony be in town or is there travel involved?"

"The ceremony's in Anacortes." Clark recalled the conversation with his sister about the hotel. Right in the middle of the historic section of Anacortes, and elegant and perfect for her wedding reception. "I already have a room booked there."

"Anacortes is great," Mitch said. "Maybe we could drive out to Deception Pass if things get too intense for you. Would you like to get together today? I could meet with you as soon as half an hour."

Clark closed his eyes and squeezed his hand into a fist to keep it from shaking, the knot in his stomach returning tighter than before. "Um, sure."

"Do you want me to come to you or meet somewhere?" Mitch asked. "Sorry, but I can't host you at my place today."

"What part of town are you in?"

"Ballard."

Clark let out a deep breath and opened his eyes. "Me, too. How about we meet at Low Key Coffee by the Majestic Bay Theater?"

"Sounds good. How will I know you?"

"Dark hair, glasses, about five nine." Clark glanced at the wall housing his coats. "I'll be wearing a brown leather jacket."

"Okay, half an hour. Four-thirty it is. I look forward to meeting you."

"See you soon." The mobile beeped twice, ending the call, and the knot in Clark's stomach released.

With a glance around the room, he decided to tidy up in case he wanted to bring Mitch back to the apartment. He did a quick clean of the bathroom and changed the sheets on the bed. Once finished, he glanced at his cell. Ten after four. Taking one last look around, he assessed the room. Much cleaner than usual. He slipped on his jacket. A smile played across his lips as he stepped out of the doorway and left his building.

He strode along Market Street, stopped at an ATM to grab three hundred in cash, just in case, and arrived at the coffee shop in less than twenty minutes. Opening the door, he gasped. Though the shop teemed with people, Clark zeroed in immediately on the man waiting for him. Across the room, the redheaded escort sat at a small table and sipped his drink. The pictures hadn't come close to doing the man justice.

Stuffing his hands into his pockets to keep them from shaking, he approached the handsome stranger and willed his knees not to give out. "Are you Mitch?"

Mitch lifted his gaze and smiled. His perfect teeth gleamed in the light of the coffee shop. "You must be Clark," the deep voice rumbled. He rose and extended his hand. "It's a pleasure to meet you."

Clark took Mitch's large hand and met the blue-eyed gaze of the escort. Though sparks didn't immediately fly though their connection, Clark drank in the man before him. "You're even hotter in person."

Mitch squeezed Clark's hand with an easy laugh.

"Thanks. You're pretty fine yourself."

Heat rose in Clark's cheeks. "Nah, I'm plain as a piece of white bread."

Continuing to hold his hand, Mitch's gaze intensified, making Clark's already precarious position regarding his knees worse. "No, you're not. I love green eyes, and I'd kiss those gorgeous full lips if we weren't in the middle of a busy coffee shop."

As he withdrew his hand, Clark's body burned with a mixture of embarrassment and desire. "That's sweet of you to say." His companion pulled out a chair at the table and, as Clark sat down, pushed it in.

"What would you like to drink?" he asked, crouching down to Clark's level. "It's on me."

Clark looked into Mitch's sapphire gaze. "Americano, two shots, no room." His voice trembled slightly, stomach knotting tighter. "Please."

Mitch grinned. "Coming right up."

He watched Mitch's round ass pushing against the fabric of his tight blue jeans after the redhead stood and made his way to the counter. Just as the man was about to order, he turned and winked. Clark smiled and shifted his gaze to the table, caught out and flushing with embarrassment. *He's probably used to being ogled.*

He shifted his thoughts to contemplate how his family would react to this man accompanying their son to Grace's wedding. Dad would want to know all about the mysterious man, and Mom would introduce him around to all the family like their wedding was the next week.

Grace would be all over him about where he'd found

such a great guy and why she hadn't met him yet. The thought did nothing to quell his nerves. Hopefully, the wedding would distract her from asking too many questions.

Still, Mitch would be a vast improvement over the last serious relationship he'd had. *Or thought I had.* Clark let out a huff. Jordan had seemed like he was 'the one'. Educated, employed, sexy as hell, and hung like a horse. He could speak with Clark's father on a range of subjects, and he'd even joined Clark's mother a few times with her card playing. Grace had adored him.

A year in, and after they'd pledged to be monogamous, Jordan got antsy and had an affair. And then another. And another. Finally, the guy admitted to Clark he'd fucked around with five men during the last six months of their relationship and left him for a hockey player. Jordan's last words still rang in Clark's ear. "I can't compete with your kids and your job."

The succession of men who followed were, by and large, quick fucks or one-night stands. Not even a friend with benefits.

Returning with their drinks, Mitch handed him the warm paper cup. "Here you go."

With a shake of his head, Clark dispelled the thoughts of his ex. "Thanks."

Mitch took his seat and set his coffee on the small table. "Tell me about this wedding." He flashed a megawatt smile. "Why is such a handsome man hiring an escort? I'm surprised there aren't several guys begging you for a date."

Shifting his gaze from his coffee, Clark settled his attention on the man stoking the butterflies in his stomach. "I've been single for a while now. It's hard to date these days, and I haven't really found the right one. Seems like every guy I've gone out with in the last year only wants to fuck, and then doesn't return my calls and texts." *Good Lord, did I just tell this guy I'm horrible in bed?*

The escort arched an eyebrow. "So, you want to hire someone?"

He blew out a breath. "Don't get me wrong, the sex is fine. It's just none of them call me back. All they looked for was a quick fuck. I'm not sure I'd want to introduce many of them to the family anyway. Not that there's *been* that many." He shrugged. "I just don't want to show up alone to my sister's wedding. Someone will try to matchmake."

"Hmm," Mitch frowned. "Are there some acceptance issues with your family?"

With a nervous laugh, Clark shook his head. "Far from it. Everyone's fine with me being gay. They're just worried I'm never going to find Mister Right. Weddings are the worst place for family judgment, even with a family as great as mine." His lips curled into a grin. "Besides, I want to make my new homophobic brother-in-law squirm."

A matching grin played across Mitch's lips. "I see. Well, the first question is, am I what you're looking for?" he asked, his intensely blue gaze locking with Clark's.

Fighting to keep his rapidly growing erection from tenting his jeans, Clark thought back to the qualifications on Mitch's ad. "You said in your post that you're able to hold your own in a conversation."

"Yup. I have a degree, and I'm well-read." He wriggled his eyebrows. "Definitely more to me than just the fun part."

Clark cleared his throat. "Speaking of which…"

"No worries there. I get checked over once a month, only play wrapped, and am on PrEP." He sat back in the chair, holding Clark with his stunning blue eyes. "And how about you?"

With a nod, Clark chuckled. "I haven't had anyone since my last checkup about a month ago, and I tested all clear. Like I said, I've sort of given up on the dating scene."

"I think you just haven't found the right guy yet. He's out there." Mitch took a sip of his coffee and set the cup on the table. "How about we head back to your place," he said, his voice deepening. "I can show you some of the services you'd be engaging."

"Sure." Clark clutched the side of the table and forced a smile as the butterflies intensified. If he'd custom-designed a boyfriend, Mitch couldn't have been more perfect. He certainly seemed like someone his father would get along with and his mother would swoon over.

Maybe escorts were naturally attractive in both their personalities and their features, but Clark *liked* the man across the table. He'd expected this arrangement to be a mere transaction, maybe with a little fun on the side. But Mitch Hampton exuded kindness, intelligence, and gentlemanly behavior. From a parade of losers to the perfect guy in one internet ad. The speed of the change in his fortunes left him reeling.

With a furrow of his brow, Mitch laid his beefy hand over Clark's. "You okay?"

Clark nodded. "Yeah, just a little nervous."

"Don't be. I won't bite." He wriggled his eyebrow, giving a little nod. "Maybe just a little nibble."

With a laugh, Clark patted the hand covering his. "Let's go."

Mitch jumped up, and as Clark rose, he pulled out the chair.

"You're quite the gentleman," Clark observed, enjoying the attention.

"Thank you," Mitch replied and swept his arm toward the exit. "After you."

They tossed the remains of their coffee into the compost bin, and Mitch held the door for him. They stepped into the bright, spring sunshine.

Strolling down Market Street, Mitch turned to Clark. "Do you live far from here?"

"About a fifteen-minute walk."

Gently grasping Clark's hand, Mitch gave it a little squeeze. "And how long has Ballard been home?"

"I've lived in Seattle about ten years, but I'm originally from Bellingham. Where are you from?" The thumb rubbing along the side of his finger made him a bit self-conscious, but as he glanced around, no one seemed to be paying them the slightest attention.

"A small town in Idaho. I think there were twenty in my graduating class." Mitch laced their fingers together. "I came to Seattle about five years ago but lived in Chicago before that."

Clark turned toward him, the tightness of his nerves relaxing under the continued handhold and rubbing thumb. "Have you been, um, escorting long?"

Mitch nodded. "About eight years, and I'm really enjoying it. I love the sex for the most part, even with the curious and the inexperienced guys, but I also enjoy meeting people and finding out why they hire an escort."

Clark cocked his head. "What has your research shown?"

"A variety of reasons. Some are unable to find people to have sex with. Some are closeted or married and want someone discreet." He gave Clark a sideway glance, his lips turning up in a grin. "Others don't want to go through the hassle of looking and find it easier to hire someone."

Curiosity overrode Clark's nervous state. "Do any of your clients hire you just for your company?"

"A few, though not many. I've escorted a few guys to office parties and just out to dinner." He squeezed Clark's hand again. "Most of them decided they wanted to take me home afterward, though."

"Do you have a lot of clients?" Clark tensed, the words tumbling out of his mouth before he had a moment to think. "Sorry, that's none of my business."

"No, it's fine," Mitch replied. "I keep my client base small. That's why I asked if you wanted to meet. I wanted to be sure you were a good match and not a psycho."

"How do you know I'm not a psych? You've only just met me," Clark retorted.

Mitch laughed. "I've been around the block a few

times. Psychos make themselves known pretty quickly. You *definitely* don't fall into that category."

"Just guys?" Clark blurted out, not entirely sure he wanted to hear the answer.

Mitch nodded. "I'm not wired for women, and I wouldn't want to disappoint anyone."

With a strange feeling of relief, Clark nodded in agreement, contemplating Mitch's life and thinking how confident his line of work had made him. Clark couldn't imagine inviting himself into a new client's bed for a 'look-see'. "Have you ever accompanied someone to a wedding?" he asked, intentionally shifting the conversation.

"A couple of times. One guy was in a position like you, but his family wasn't as accepting. I was moral support. The other was a groom, and we shared the other groom on their wedding night."

Clark's jaw dropped. "You had a threesome with the couple getting married?"

Mitch chuckled. "Yup. That was quite a weekend."

Contemplating the image of Mitch sharing a wedding bed with two grooms, Clark had to adjust the firmness forming in his pants with his free hand. Mitch continued to laugh but didn't say anything further until they reached the entrance of Clark's building.

With reluctance, because he'd liked how his hand felt held inside Mitch's, he slipped his fingers free to reach into his pocket, retrieve his key, and unlock the main door.

Mitch looked around as they made their way toward the elevator. "Nice. Looks like it was built in the 1930's."

"Very good," Clark replied, impressed with either

Mitch's guess or knowledge of architecture. "1932." The doors were open, and they stepped inside.

"Classic design," Mitch commented, looking around the lobby. "I love it."

They stood in the elevator slightly apart until the door closed.

Mitch faced him, stepping closer with an unmistakable hunger clouding his eyes. "May I kiss you?"

His face inches away, Clark swallowed, his nerves returning. "Yes."

Mitch placed a hand on Clark's cheek and drew him closer, their lips meeting. His eyes closed. A soft moan accompanied the rush of warmth while the kiss grew from gentle exploration to full passion.

The elevator dinged, and they pulled apart as the car slowed to a halt. Clark took a shaky couple of steps, still reeling from the intensity of their kiss.

"Gonna make it, or should I carry you?" Mitch drawled.

"A tempting offer," Clark smiled, "but I can make it on my own." He found his footing and led Mitch to his apartment door. Fumbling with the keys, he caught the jangling metal before they fell to the floor. "Damn it."

"Let me." Mitch took the keys from him and opened the door. He pulled Clark in and pressed him against the wall as the door slammed shut. "I wanted you the first moment I saw you." He ran his tongue from Clark's collar to his right ear.

"Oh, fuck," Clark gasped, goosebumps running along his arms and legs.

Mitch nibbled on his earlobe then whispered in his ear, "Are you a top or a bottom?"

"Usually top," he breathed.

With a last nibble, the escort kissed down his neck. "Good." Wrapping his arms around Clark's body, Mitch engulfed him in his muscular embrace, trailed his warm hands down Clark's back, and dipped beneath the waistband of his jeans. "You're sexy." The escort gave each cheek a squeeze while he slid his firm body down Clark's until he was kneeling. Seductive fingers caressed the aching bulge pressing against the unyielding denim.

Mitch's blue eyes stared up and locked with Clark's. He unbuckled Clark's belt and pulled open the button, offering some relief to the fully hard erection trapped inside the tight jeans. He slowly slid the zipper down, licking the fabric covering the shaft. "Do you want me to suck you?"

"Yes." Clark breathed, using the wall to hold himself up.

"Do you want to shoot on me?"

More goosebumps surged up Clark's legs and back. The image of Mitch's chest covered in his load flashed across his mind. His gaze wandered to the small of Mitch's back, a light dusting of red hair covering the exposed skin between T-shirt and jeans. "I'd rather fuck your sweet ass."

Mitch grinned. "On the wedding weekend, we can do both."

Running his fingers through Mitch's soft red hair, Clark made his decision. "We'll have to actually attend the ceremony."

With a chuckle, Mitch kissed along the length of the hard shaft. "Yeah, but we'll have each night to ourselves—unless you want to invite some of the other guests to join us."

Clark's cock pulsed at the idea of sharing another of the wedding guests with his companion.

"I see you like that idea." Mitch tugged the jeans down Clark's hips and freed his aching dick from his boxer-briefs, engulfing the head into his mouth.

When Mitch slipped his tongue under the foreskin, jolts of pleasure surged through Clark's body. "Yeah, so good."

Mitch hummed, the vibrations massaging Clark's erection. With his knees weakening, Clark placed a hand on Mitch's shoulder to keep upright and eased the sucking lips from his cock. "We need to take this to the bedroom, or I'll fall over."

He took Mitch's hand, pulled him to his feet, then hiked up his jeans enough to enable him to walk. They moved farther into the apartment and through the French doors to the bedroom. Without a word, Clark pushed him onto the bed and shed his clothes, standing naked before his hired man.

Mitch's jaw dropped, his eyes widening. "Whoa."

Suddenly self-conscious, Clark looked down at his body. "What's wrong?"

With a shake of his head, the escort let out a low whistle. "Nothing wrong at all. You're beautiful. I love the hair pattern across your chest." He jumped off the bed and quickly stripped, the muscles of his hairless chest flexing and stretching when he moved his arms. The rich colors of the toucan on his shoulder contrasted with his light tan.

Now Clark's jaw dropped. "You're even more ripped than in your photos." He ran his fingers over the eight-pack of Mitch's abs and grazed the trimmed hairs above the rock-hard cock. Pressing his body against Mitch's, he savored the warmth coming off the muscular man and kissed him deeply.

Clark ran his hands lightly over the short hairs covering the perfect globes of Mitch's ass, eliciting a moan from him.

"I can't wait until you slide inside me." Mitch wrapped his arms around Clark, and they tumbled onto the comforter, continuing to kiss.

Rolling on top, Clark licked and nibbled his way down Mitch's neck and swirled his tongue around the erect nubs protruding from the sculpted chest. He grazed his teeth across the hardened nipples.

Mitch's back arched. "Oh, fuck, I love nip work."

After a few more nibbles and licks, Clark released one nipple and kissed his way to the other. Mitch's cock jumped and pressed into Clark's stomach. Grabbing the escort's shoulders, Clark slid forward, bringing his lips to Mitch's neck.

"Geez," Mitch gasped, both fists clutching the sheet. "You're a master at this."

"I get inspired when I have a gorgeous man like you in my bed." Clark licked and kissed back down Mitch's chest and followed the thin trail of hair below the bellybutton to the prize he sought. He gripped the shaft, marveling at the length and thickness. "You've got an amazing cock." He pressed his lips against the cut head and probed his tongue lightly against the opening at the tip.

Mitch's body convulsed as he threw back his head, his mouth wide open. "Ahhh…"

Clark sucked in the entire shaft, pressing his nose into the trimmed red hairs at the root. Not wanting to gag and ruin the moment, Clark backed off, keeping more than half of Mitch's cock in his mouth, and put his tongue to work swirling around the head.

"Amazing," Mitch moaned.

A slight musk radiated from beneath the large balls, and Clark inhaled and tightened his lips to increase the suction. Pulling off the shaft, he licked the space between Mitch's balls and leg, eliciting another gasp from the writhing man. Clark pushed the escort's legs up and licked along the trimmed space between heavy balls and the tight puckered entrance of his luscious ass.

Clark licked around the hole, lightly biting the flesh of Mitch's firm globes. He pressed Mitch's legs against his chest, exposing the hole to the ceiling. Curling his tongue, Clark pressed against the tight opening.

Mitch slammed his hands onto the bed and grabbed the comforter in his large fists. "Oh, fuck. Your tongue's amazing."

Varying between lapping and prodding, Clark worked over the clean ass until Mitch settled his legs on Clark's shoulders and gently pushed him back.

"I could happily shoot just like this," Mitch said with heavy breath. "But I want that big cock of yours inside me."

Stretching his body over Mitch's, Clark grazed his dick along the saliva-slickened crevice. Mitch's legs wrapped around Clark's torso, and his heels settled on Clark's ass. Reaching over and opening the drawer of his nightstand, Clark retrieved a bottle of lube and a condom.

Returning to his position between Mitch's legs, he rolled the rubber over his shaft and applied lube. He drizzled more of the slick liquid onto Mitch's pucker and pressed a finger into the hole to lube inside. Mitch sucked in a breath.

"Okay?" Clark asked, continuing to move his finger inside Mitch. He swiped at the hard nugget of the man's prostate.

"Yeah, good," he grunted, then relaxed. "So good."

Slowly removing his digit, Clark placed the head of his covered shaft against the pucker and locked his gaze with Mitch's. "Ready?"

With a nod, he pressed back against Clark. "Please slide it in me."

Exquisite tightness grasped Clark's cock as he slowly slid inside the moaning stud. "Doing okay?"

Mitch's features were taut with desire. "Don't stop. I want it all."

Bottoming out, Clark paused to give Mitch a moment to get used to his size. Mitch dug his heels into his ass. "Take me as hard as you want. Your cock feels amazing."

Clark pulled most of the way out and slowly pressed back inside. He repeated the gentle motion several times, increasing his speed and intensity. Soon, he pounded

Mitch hard and fast as the escort gripped the sheets. "Show me what you've got."

Before long, the tingle started in Clark's balls, ratcheting up the desperate urgency. He pounded the redhead harder and stroked the man's fully erect shaft in time to his thrusts. Mitch's back arched, his mouth rounded, and several long blasts of come sprayed across his abs. The tightly squeezing sphincter accompanying the escort's orgasm took Clark over the edge. With one final thrust, he shuddered as his load pumped into the rubber lodged deep inside Mitch's quivering ass.

Panting, Clark fell forward, a gooey mess pressing against his chest.

While Clark rested and caught his breath, Mitch wrapped his arm around Clark's back and traced lazy patterns along his spine. Mitch's heartbeat, slowing back to normal, thudded against Clark's cheek and ear.

Reluctantly, Clark slid his softening cock out of Mitch's ass.

Mitch pulled him up for a kiss. "I haven't been fucked like that in a long time." He pressed his lips against Clark's cheek. "Thank you."

Clark nestled his chin into the crook of Mitch's neck. For a few moments, he reveled in the warmth of the man beside him. Then he lifted his head, not wanting their time together to end. "Would you like a glass of wine?"

With a yawn, Mitch eased himself up to sit. "Sounds great. Thank you."

"Let me get us a washcloth as well." Clark tugged off the condom and pushed himself off the bed. A slight rush of dizziness made him sway, and he reached out for the side of the bed, nearly dropping the condom.

Mitch reached across the bed and clutched his hand. "You okay?"

The dizziness cleared after he blinked his eyes a couple of times. "Fine. Just a little head rush." He met Mitch's gaze. "I'll be right back."

He stepped out of the room and across the hall to the bathroom. Opening the cabinet door, he grabbed a washcloth and ran the water until it warmed.

After wiping himself down and rinsing out the cloth, he returned and handed the rag to Mitch.

"Thanks." Mitch ran the washcloth over his chest, clearing away the mess from their coupling. Clark watched the washcloth gliding along the smooth skin and kicked himself for not offering to clean Mitch off.

Clark took the cloth back as Mitch moved off the bed, and both men found their underwear. After tossing the damp rag in the bathroom sink, Clark scurried into the kitchen while Mitch followed. Grabbing a couple of glasses and a bottle of wine from the counter, he led his guest into the living room. Seated, he popped the cork and poured them each a glass.

From the armchair, Mitch raised his, swirled the wine, sniffed, and took a sip. He nodded. "This is delightful."

"It's a white merlot," Clark said, holding the glass at an angle and noting the yellow hue of the light passing through the wine.

After swirling the glass and taking a sip, Mitch hummed in appreciation. "I love it."

Clark's cock stirred again when he glanced at the strong, splayed legs. His gaze followed along tightly muscled thighs, over perfectly defined abs and chest, and finally settled onto the handsome face of the man he'd just shared his bed with.

Mitch caught him looking, heat still in his gaze, and smiled. "I'm glad you emailed me. This afternoon has been great."

"For me, too. If you still want to come to the wedding with me, I'd love it."

"Absolutely." Mitch's smile deepened the lines beside his eyes, and then he winked. "I'm looking forward to spending a weekend with you."

A soft chime floated across the room. Mitch set his wineglass on the coffee table and stood. "Sorry." He hurried into the bedroom and returned carrying his clothes. "I need to get going. I have an appointment at eight."

Clark glanced at his watch. Seven-thirty. "Wow, how did it get that late?"

A grin played across Mitch's lips. "Time flies when we're having fun."

"Do you want a quick shower?" Clark offered, gesturing toward the bathroom.

Mitch shook his head. "I'm okay. It's not another client."

Clark wondered why Mitch felt the need to reassure him but was pleased nonetheless.

Mitch slid on his clothes and smoothed his hair. "So, let me know about the arrangements."

Clark stood and set his glass on the end table. "I'll pick you up at your place mid-morning, and we'll head north."

"Great." Mitch closed the last button of his shirt, and then moved closer to slip his arms around Clark. "It was a pleasure to meet you."

"Hang on a minute." Clark pulled away and retrieved the money he'd grabbed from the ATM. "Don't forget this."

"Two-fifty is fine."

He handed two hundred-sixty to Mitch.

"That's sweet of you." After pocketing the payment, Mitch kissed him. "I really enjoyed our time together. You'd be able to get any man to go to this wedding, you know."

Heat rose into Clark's cheeks. "You sure know how to flatter a guy."

Mitch narrowed his gaze. "I mean it. You're amazing. See you soon." Mitch kissed him one last time and stepped through the door. "Bye." He waved and headed down the hall.

Clark closed the door, rested his back against it, and smiled. *I just hired an escort to accompany me to my sister's wedding...*

CHAPTER TWO

TWO WEEKS LATER, Clark balanced Firestone House's checking account. He'd just celebrated his seventh year with the non-profit foundation for gay youth and loved every minute of his job helping kids who had nowhere else to go. He'd just clicked SAVE when his cell rang. His sister's smiling face lit up the screen, and he accepted the call. "Hey, sis. Are you still going through with this wedding?"

He could almost hear her eyes rolling. "I already told you I am. Dan's..." she paused, "a work in process. I wish you could see him at his best. He's really a great guy."

"As you're well aware, Grace, that has not been my experience with him." Though he'd had a grand total of two interactions with Dan Palucinski, neither had been good. Grace's fiancé didn't like gay guys, and he'd made no secret of his displeasure at finding his future brother-in-law was an out and proud gay man. Unfortunately, his sister was completely smitten, and no amount of cajoling or reasoning by Clark or their parents could sway her from accepting Dan's marriage proposal.

"I know, Clark. But that's not what I called about." She clicked her tongue. "Do you have a date yet for the wedding? I need to know for the caterer."

He shook his head, knowing full well she wanted to set him up with someone. "Sure, that's the reason…"

"It is," she squealed. "It's not the *only* reason, but it's the *primary* reason I'm asking."

"Oh, God, here it comes…" He closed the spreadsheet on his computer, deliberately making his sister wait.

"I can hear you clicking and typing. I'm guessing that means you *have* a date you don't want to tell me about, or you *don't* have a date and are trying to stall my matchmaking."

Well, shit. His sister had an uncanny way of reading him, even over the phone. If he told her yes, he'd have to come up with some sort of description of his date. At this point, that was Mitch the escort, and he wanted to make her wait for that unveiling.

"I'm waiting…" she said, her voice cooing. "You can tell me. Does he have some sort of issue? Tiny dick or something adorably sad?"

"Maybe I shouldn't bring a date," he shot back. "What would your beloved think of me kissing on some guy at his party?"

She sighed. "He already knows you're bringing a date, and that your date will be a guy."

He huffed. "I notice you didn't say he was cool with it."

"Doesn't matter," she replied, unfazed. "If he *isn't* cool with it, I'm not marrying him."

"Might be worth bringing some hottie and making out with him in the pews just to see his reaction."

"Clark Adamson, don't you dare ruin my wedding!" She shrieked through the cell.

He chuckled. "It wouldn't be ruined for me." He considered how to answer her question. For now, the safe response seemed prudent. "Okay, here's the deal. I asked Roger, you know, my college roommate...?"

"Oh, I'd love to see Roger again," she gushed. "He's such a sweetie. Weren't you two dating or something?"

"We had a fling when we were in college, but nothing serious." He remembered their study sessions, most of which had ended up with him on his back. "That reminds me. I need to call him and see if his company hired an assistant for him."

"Focus. You asked Roger to be your date, but..." she led.

"But his boyfriend got shot. Paul's a cop."

Grace gasped. "Is he okay?"

"He is, but Roger and Paul's sister have been taking care of him." He chuckled again. "And when I say taking care of him, I mean keeping him from overexerting himself and trying to escape the condo. It's like taking care of a hyperactive kid being forced to sit still."

She laughed. "I can imagine you'd be just as bad."

With a shrug, he glanced out the window to see a police cruiser pull up. "Hey, I gotta go. I think we're getting a new street kid, and I want to talk to the officer."

"Okay, I'll make sure the caterer knows you're bringing a date. If it's not Roger, you'd better tell me all about the guy you find."

"Gotta go, Grace," he said hurriedly. "Bye." He ended

the call before she could interrogate him further and pushed up from his chair.

He recognized the officer getting out of the car as Officer Jason Lynch, Paul Tomlinson's beat partner. With a sigh, he headed to the front office. Jason wasn't his favorite person since he'd had a run-in with Roger a few weeks back. Roger had forgiven him, but Clark didn't take kindly to any abusive behavior, especially focused on his best friend. Still, the man brought in kids needing help, and that's what his foundation was there for.

Jason led a disheveled young man into the room with a firm hand on his shoulder. "Hi, Clark. Thought I'd see Justine here."

"She's off on a family emergency," Clark said, explaining why his intake coordinator wasn't there. "I'm pulling double-duty now."

"Gotcha," he said with a grin. He nodded at the street kid. "This is Tanner. I found him under the South Park Bridge."

Focusing on the young man, Clark looked him over. Dark hair, likely a mix of Southeast Asian and European descent, and a slight build. The trembling kid glanced back and forth between Clark and the officer.

Clark gave the kid a small smile. "Hi, Tanner. Welcome to Firestone House." He stuck out his hand.

Not surprisingly, the kid didn't take it, flinching backward instead. He hugged his arms around himself and stared at Jason. "Why did you bring me here? I thought you were arresting me."

"Nope," Jason said. "Shake Clark's hand. He's here to

help you."

Tentatively reaching out his hand, Tanner's delicate fingers wrapped around Clark's. "What am I doing here?"

Clark shook then let go. "We help LGBTQ kids who have no-where else to go. I'm assuming you're gay?"

Flinching again, Tanner darted his gaze between Jason and Clark but didn't answer.

"Don't worry, Tanner," Jason said with a soothing tone. "Clark and I are both gay. We're not out to bash you or anything."

"Y…you are?" He stared in awe at Jason.

The officer chuckled. "Sure am. My husband and I have been together for six years now."

"You have nothing to be scared of," Clark assured him. "We just want to help."

Tanner visibly relaxed, though kept a skeptical frown on his face. "Why would you want to help me?"

"Helping kids like you is the sole purpose of this organization. The Firestone House was founded by a wealthy philanthropist to help the huge number of LGBTQ youth out on the streets have a chance in life." Clark smiled kindly at Tanner. "We have quite a few success stories."

The young man narrowed his eyes. "What's the catch?"

"No drugs allowed," Jason piped up.

Tanner scrunched his face in disgust. "I don't do drugs, man."

"Good," Clark nodded. "That takes care of any rehab needs. So, the deal is, you stay here, finish up any high school classes you need to graduate, and then we work on college or vocational school to get you going in a career."

Clenching his fists, Tanner blanched. "I ain't got money for college, man."

Clark shrugged. "You don't need it. We have a deal with the community college for classes, and we'll work on scholarships and financial aid for any university coursework." Clark woke up the computer at the front desk and pulled up an intake form. "You'll be expected to work hard at your studies, as well as chores and such here at the house. We offer a place to stay, meals, and a warm bed."

Tanner chewed his bottom lip, still looking dubious. But at Jason's solemn nod, and Clark's steady smile, his frown eased. Realization dawned on his face. "You're really gonna help me?" he asked, his voice softening in wonderment.

Clark nodded. "If you keep up your end of the deal, you'll get an education. It'll be hard work, but you'll be off the streets. You won't have to worry about hunger or the cold. You'll be safe here. What do you think?"

With his brown eyes wide, Tanner turned to Jason. "Is this for real?"

"Yeah, kid. You were in the right place, and the right cop found you." Jason's stare hardened. "I only bring kids here I think will take advantage of the help offered. Don't prove me wrong about you."

Returning his gaze to Clark, Tanner thought for a moment. "Okay, I'll try it out."

"Good," Jason said. "I'll get your stuff from the cruiser."

Tanner wrapped his arms around himself again, nerves

on clear display, and his face tightening. Clark wasn't sure, but he thought the kid might be trying not to cry.

After Jason left the room, Clark came around the counter and stood before Tanner. "Ready to get started?"

Tanner nodded with a sniffle. "Sorry," he said, his voice choking. "I've been on my own for a long time."

Clark smiled, patting him on the shoulder. "Let's get the paperwork taken care of, and I'll show you up to your room."

BUOYED BY THE marketing plan he'd received from the contracted firm, Wes Palucinski strode into his boss's office. "Emily, did you see the…"

Glancing up at him with the phone at her ear, she held up a finger with a long, manicured nail painted metallic blue. "Honey, I need you to find a good wine for dinner tonight with Jason and Mike."

Wes took stock of his boss's appearance. Each day seemed a new adventure in the clothing sensibilities of Emily Sanders-Gunn. Her usual red curls were pulled back into a tight bun with a pewter hat pin presumably holding the mess together. Her full make-up included light blue shadow over her eyes, and orangey-red lipstick that matched her hair. A leopard-print, low-cut blouse under a khaki linen business suit completed the picture.

Tame for Emily.

She listened to her husband's response, and her lips curved into a smile. "Just make sure it pairs with steak salad."

Wes chuckled to himself. His boss's taste in wine was legendarily bad. He turned to the window after she shot him a glare to fight a widening smile. Taking in the Seattle skyline, he tried to focus on something other than the train wreck his boss wore or the negotiation with her husband over wine. He watched a plane fly south toward Sea-Tac Airport framed by Mount Rainier.

"Sorry, I've got to go. Wes just walked in." Her voice dripped with sarcasm. "And he looks like he has something to say."

Wes turned back, barely containing his smirk.

"Love you, too." She pulled the phone away from her ear, pressed the glass screen, and lifted her narrowed gaze to Wes. "Remember, I hold the fate of your raise in my hands. Choose your words carefully."

Laughing, Wes took the seat across from her. "I'm sure your husband will make the right choice. He's a bartender, right?"

"Yup. I get constant shit from my best friend about wine. Best to let Seb handle it." She clasped her fingers together. "So, what can I do for you?"

"I want to get your trip dates on my calendar," he deadpanned, fully aware she wasn't taking a vacation.

Her brow furrowed. "What are you talking about?"

"Well, I figured you were going on safari in that outfit."

She turned in her chair, uncrossing her leg and revealing a bright orange stiletto heel.

He nodded at her shoe. "Oh, my mistake."

Shaking her head, she crossed her arms. "Is this a

fashion critique, or do you actually have something *work-*related to discuss with me?"

With a laugh, he shrugged. "Either works, but I was wondering if you'd seen the marketing plan I forwarded from McKenzie Wright?" Wes's smile faded, nerves taking over. "I think it's pretty good, but I wanted your opinion before I gave the final authorization."

Emily turned to her computer and started clicking with the mouse. After staring at the screen for a few moments, she returned her gaze to Wes. "Do you think this is the correct messaging?"

With a nod, Wes glanced at the screen. "The online training courses we're trying to sell need to appeal to a wide audience. I think McKenzie captured the right tone in the campaign, and the customers should respond to the tagline."

Returning her attention to the screen, Emily clicked through a few more pages of the presentation. "I like the graphics, and the detail is impressive."

Wes leaned forward. "So, we're good to go?" He'd been working with McKenzie Wright, a graphic designer and marketing assistant with Herrington, Fisher, and Scallione for the better part of a year to get the right message together. If Emily thought it was ready to launch, he'd put the project to bed and move on to the next stage.

"I say go for it." She grinned. "You've done a great job, Wes. You'll see a bonus on your next payroll."

His eyes widened. "Bonus?"

"I recognize good work, and you've been pretty tireless in your pursuit of this project." She pulled open her calendar. "Though, the amount was higher before you came in."

He grinned. "Professional hazard."

"I'm also authorizing a week off for you," she continued. "Isn't your brother's wedding coming up soon?"

"Yeah," he said, a bit of dread scarring what should have been a happy moment.

Emily raised an eyebrow. "You don't seem too excited about it."

"I'm not," he grumbled. "But I appreciate the time off. There's a bunch of stuff to get together before the wedding. The ceremony's in Anacortes, and I'll have to go up there a few days beforehand to chat with the owner of the pub I want to rent for the bachelor party." He wrinkled his nose. "I'm the best man."

She frowned. "So, what's the problem?" Raking an appraising gaze over him, she gave a sly smile. "Or is it the frumpy-gay look you've got going on today bringing you down?"

"We can't all look like we're hunting wild beasts," Wes retorted. He let out a sigh. "I don't have a date, and my brother's going to be relentless about wanting to hook me up at the wedding."

Emily shrugged. "I still don't see the problem. Isn't there a hot guy or two coming to the wedding? He was in a frat, wasn't he?"

"Uh," Wes hesitated. "I'm not *out* to my family."

"Why not?" She scrunched her forehead. "You're out at work. That guy you brought to the Christmas party would make a great date for the wedding. Your folks would swoon over that head of red hair and all those muscles."

He barked out a laugh. "Hardly. My mother would hemorrhage something if she found out I'm gay. Doesn't mix well with my parents' religion."

"Well, shit, Wes. That must not make your life very easy." She puffed out a breath. "Let me know if I can help."

Shaking his head, he let out another sigh. "Sadly, I'm on my own with this one. Who knows? Maybe there'll be a nice, single, handsome, and closeted guy there I can hook up with."

She grinned. "One can hope. It's kind of a requirement to hook up with someone at a wedding, you know."

His phone buzzed against his leg, and he fished it from his pocket. The patented scowl of his mother's face covered the screen. "Speak of the devil..." He glanced up at his boss. "Mind if I take this?"

She turned back to her screen. "Go ahead. Let McKenzie know the campaign is ready to go."

"Thanks, Emily." He jumped up from the chair and accepted the call as he strode from the room. "Hello?"

"Wesley, dear. It's mom." Her voice held the same tinge of anger and disdain he associated with much of his childhood.

He cringed. "Hi. Is anything wrong?"

"Yes. I'm holding a dinner to meet Grace's family, and she informs me that her gay brother is attending." She snorted. "Imagine, one of those gays in *my* dining room? What will the church say?"

A flush of angry heat rose up Wes's neck. "What business is it of your church people?"

"If you'd attend church like I raised you to do, you'd understand how important it is to keep your brothers and sisters in Christ close to your side."

Feeling the old familiar weight of his secret on the back of his neck, he shook his head. "Okay, I'm at work," he said, his tone short. He stepped into his office and nudged the door closed with his shoe. "What does your dinner have to do with me?"

"*Our* dinner, Wesley," she corrected. "The whole family is hosting, and you'll be attending."

He stopped short at the edge of his desk. "What? I don't want to come to some dinner party with Grace's parents."

"Of course, you do. I need you here to help me welcome the Adamsons into the family." Her tone turned nasty. "Just stay away from the gay. He'll try to turn you to his wicked ways."

"This behavior right here is why I don't want to come." He continued around his desk and sat in his office chair. "I don't buy into your judgements."

"Wesley!" she screeched. "You'll be respectful to your mother."

He rolled his eyes, backing down. The last thing he wanted right now, besides attending his brother's wedding, was another argument with his mother about her views. "What day is the party?"

"Tomorrow," she crowed in triumph. "Be here at five to help."

"Okay," he huffed. "Want me to bring anything?"

His mother didn't miss a beat with her frosty tone. "Just yourself, since you still aren't married to a nice, young lady."

His hand slapped against the desktop as he fought not to scream at her. "I'll be there," he snapped, then ended the call. *I'm going for a drink tonight, and maybe I'll call that hot red-head Emily mentioned.*

CLARK STRODE INTO the reception area of Firestone House bright and early the next morning to find Tanner standing next to Clark's office door. "Hey, Tanner. Good morning."

Tanner kicked the toe of his grubby shoe into the floor. "Um, hi."

Sliding the key into the lock of his office door, Clark stared curiously at the young man. "Can I do something for you?"

Another kick. "The office lady said you were an accountant."

"Yes, I am." He opened the door. "Want to come inside?"

"Sure." Tanner shuffled past him, his head down.

Clark followed him in, noting his clean hoodie and jeans, and his freshly washed hair. Justine had returned to the House the previous evening and must have taken charge of Tanner's care.

"Have a seat." Clark gestured to one of the overstuffed chairs he'd insisted on having. He'd found the usual office chairs made the kids feel like they were in trouble.

"Thanks." Tanner sat and fidgeted with his fingers.

"I'm guessing you're not having problems with your tax returns." He grinned. "That's usually what follows 'I hear you're an accountant'."

"Nah, I'm just interested in numbers." He stared into his hands. "I liked math when I was in school."

Clark took the chair behind his desk and powered on his computer. "Oh. Would you like to do something in the business realm?"

Tanner shrugged. "Accounting sounds cool." He lifted his gaze, embarrassment and fear reflecting in his eyes. "Could you show me what you do?"

"Sure," Clark said quickly. The teens usually took a lot of time to come out of their shells and express an interest in something. "I'd be delighted."

"Yeah?" Tanner perked up, cautious excitement lighting his face.

"Absolutely. There's a lot to learn, but I could show you the basics." Clark logged in and waited for the computer to install updates.

Tanner dropped his gaze again. "I got A's in algebra before I quit school."

"Why did you quit?" Clark asked.

"My folks died, and their other son threw me out," he muttered. "I was adopted."

Focusing his attention on Tanner, Clark shook his head. "Wasn't there anyone around to help you?"

"Brady told them all I was a thief and a liar." He sighed. "And that I'm gay. Everyone turned their backs on me. I had to leave town."

"What town?"

"Steptoe," he nearly spat the name. "It's out in Eastern Washington."

Clark nodded, remembering the road trip he'd taken around the state with Roger after graduation. "I know where it is. On the way to Pullman from Spokane."

"Yeah. Just a grain silo, a gas station, and a graveyard," Tanner huffed.

"What happened to you after you left town?"

"Had enough for a bus ticket to Bellingham." His brow furrowed. "My brother took everything, but I'd heard that Western had a program for teens."

Clark furrowed his brow. "The university? I haven't heard of anything like that."

Tanner shook his head. "That's because there wasn't one. The lady at the administration office said to come back when I graduate high school. I didn't have anywhere to go."

"So, you came down to Seattle?" Clark asked, encouraging Tanner to go on.

"No. I met up with this older kid, and we looked out for each other." Tanner scratched a spot on his head. "Kelton wouldn't come with me when I decided to come down here from Bellingham."

The update restarted the computer, and Clark huffed. "I hate these updates." He turned back to Tanner. "When was the last time you saw him?"

"About a year ago. His old man threw him out, and he hitched a ride from Ellensburg."

A frown pulled at Clark's lips. "I'm sorry to hear that. It sounds like you two got close."

"I thought we were. But he loved some other guy." Tanner shrugged. "Maybe that's why he didn't come with me to Seattle." Sadness flashed across his face, and the corners of his mouth turned downward.

Sensing the young man he'd left behind meant more to him than the shrug suggested, Clark decided not to press for too many details. Hopefully, the more comfortable Tanner felt, the more he'd eventually open up.

The computer finished the update, and a reminder popped up when he opened his email. His brow furrowed, and he let out a puff of breath. "Shit."

"Something wrong?" Tanner asked, a fearful tone to his voice.

Clark glanced over, noting Tanner's tense posture. "Nothing for you to worry about. I forgot about a dinner I have to go to tonight."

Letting go of the arms of the chair, the young man relaxed. "Oh. Is it bad?"

"My sister's future in-laws. She's getting married in a couple weeks." His mind drifted to Mitch, wondering if he should check in with his date.

"What's wrong with them?"

Tanner's question brought him back to their conversation. Clark opened the accounting software for the House. "My sister's fiancé doesn't like gay guys."

Tanner's brows lowered. "But your sister's going to marry him? Is she okay with gay guys?"

Nodding, Clark let out a chuckle. "She's been trying

to set me up on dates since we were in high school. No problem with her." He gave an exaggerated shudder. "I don't get what she sees in him, and I guess his parents are worse than he is."

"Sounds like my brother." Tanner crossed his arms over his chest. "Don't go to the dinner. You're really nice, and you shouldn't go where people will be shitty to you."

A smile inched across Clark's lips. "Well, thank you, Tanner. If something goes bad, I'll leave, but I've got to support my sister. She's amazing."

"I wish my brother had been like you." He dipped his head again.

Clark's heart broke for the abandoned young man. "How about I show you some accounting, and then we can grab lunch and talk about what it takes to be an accountant."

Tanner met his gaze. Glimmers of trust and excitement shone in his eyes. "Thanks."

Chapter Three

WES HAD TO fight hard not to throw his mother's wedding china onto the dining room table while he listened to his parents discussing the impending dinner with the Adamsons.

"To think, I have to have one of those *gays* in my home." His mother's voice pierced the calm of the house, repeating the line she'd spouted several times in the last hour he'd been there.

Cringing, Wes set the last of the plates on the table. He'd avoided family dinners over the last five years, having tired of his family's homophobia. For some reason, they just couldn't stop discussing the subject—a topic made worse when the marriage equality bill had passed in Washington State. Both of his parents had lost their shit when the Supreme Court upheld the law.

His mother marched into the dining room with two fistfuls of silverware. For whatever reason, she'd chosen to wear her white blouse with the black buttons and frilly collar with black slacks. The gold cross of her necklace settled perfectly between the top two buttons of her blouse. The white and black ensemble made her poorly colored black, straight hair stand out, and the effect washed out her already pale face. If she hadn't been wearing her powder-blue cooking apron, she would have looked like a sickly waitress.

"The table looks nice, Wesley. Here's the silver. I see you found the wine glasses." She gave the table a once-over and frowned. "No, dear." She set the utensils on the table and plucked up one of the cloth napkins, holding it out to him with an accusatory scowl. "I told you the blue ones, not the green."

"Sorry." He took the napkin from her and calmly set it back onto the table. "There were only seven of the blue ones, and there will be eight for dinner."

"I prefer the blue." She narrowed her gaze. "We can give the gay a paper napkin."

Wes felt as though his head might explode. He rounded on her. "Let's get one thing straight, right now, Mother. Tonight, you will treat everyone at this table with respect."

Her eyes widened. "How dare you speak to me that way."

"And how dare you be ungracious to someone you've invited into this house," he spat back. "I'm sure God would welcome everyone to His table."

She spluttered and fumed as she stormed out of the room, only to be replaced a few moments later by his frowning father. He, at least, seemed to have taken the dinner seriously. He sported a tan shirt that hid the beginnings of his middle-aged paunch and complimented his thinning brown hair. The open sweater over his shirt had a pattern of large diamonds in black, white, and brown. Dark brown slacks and a pair of black dress shoes finished the ensemble.

"Wesley, you will apologize to your mother." He stern gaze accompanied his crossed arms. "This is a stressful evening for us, having one of those godless faggots in our home."

Wes held his breath while his stomach knotted. He didn't know how he was going to get through the evening. Lifting his chin, he retorted, "I'll make you a deal, Dad. I'll treat you both with the same respect you afford our guests. It's entirely up to you how this evening goes." He didn't want to be here, and his mother's behavior only made the feeling stronger. While he liked Dan's fiancée Grace, the evening had the potential to explode, and, long ago, he'd made a point of avoiding any discussion of homosexuality with his family.

Mercifully, the doorbell rang, and his father fled from the dining room. A few moments later, Dan led Grace into the dining room, followed by his scowling father. His brother stood half an inch shorter than Wes but had a stronger build. Dan resembled their mother in some ways but had a much easier-going demeanor than either parent. Wes stood impressed at the fitted navy-blue sports jacket over his white dress shirt, the top two buttons open. His slacks matched the jacket.

Dan hurried up to him and gave him a quick hug and a slap on the back. "Hey, bro. Glad you came. How's it going?"

Eyeing his father, Wes forced a smile. "Oh, it's going *great*." He turned to Grace, and his smile relaxed, turning genuine. "Hey future-sis. You look stunning tonight."

She laughed, her long, blonde hair shaking. "You're a charmer, Wes." She also gave him a hug. Stunning as ever, she wore a yellow cocktail dress, slim and fitting her curves perfectly. She glanced at the table. "This looks lovely. Can I help?"

"No, I've got it covered." He picked up the forks and began his orbit around the table. "Maybe see if Mom needs anything. She's in the kitchen."

Grace headed into the kitchen, and Dan glanced between his brother and his father, arching an eyebrow at Wes before following his fiancée.

Their father stood at the head of the table, hands clutching the back of his usual chair. "I'm warning you, Wesley…"

Wes tossed the remainder of the forks on the table with a loud clatter and placed his hands on the tall back of another chair, matching his father's posture. "I'm happy to leave now. You're the ones forcing me to be at this bullshit dinner." Though he kept his voice low, he made no effort to hide the raw edge of his anger.

Relenting, his father shook his head. "We need you to stay." He left the room grumbling.

"How nice to be wanted," Wes muttered under his breath. He resumed setting the table, placing the knives and spoons onto the green napkins. He'd just filled the last of the water glasses from the ceramic pitcher when the doorbell rang again.

His mother flew from the kitchen, untying her apron as she went. Passing through the dining room, she didn't spare him or the table a glance. A moment later, Dan and

Grace followed from the kitchen. Grace continued through, but Dan paused.

"Hey, bro. What's going on with you and Mom?" Keeping his voice low, Dan furrowed his brow. "You've got her really upset."

"I'll give you the same warning I gave her and Dad." Wes stabbed his index finger into his brother's chest. "If you're a shit to Grace's brother or her parents, I'll stand up and walk out of this house."

"Damn it, Wes. Do you have to bring up the fag right this second?" Dan scowled.

"I mean it." Wes crossed his arms, glaring at Dan. "One wrong word from you, and I'm out. You can explain to Grace why I won't show up at your wedding."

Dan threw up his hands. "Dude, I already got this from Grace in the car. Just lay off Mom and Dad, and I'll lay off Grace's gay brother."

His mother led Grace's family into the dining room. "Dan, I'm sure you already know the Adamsons." Betraying none of her earlier anger, his mother brought the guests forward. "This is our other son, Wesley."

Mrs. Adamson turned to Wes's mother. "You have such handsome boys." Her auburn hair curled next to her cheeks in a classic pageboy, highlighting her soft features. She wore a longer version of her daughter's cocktail dress, forest green with gold *fleur-de-lis.*

Wes's mother beamed with pride. "We are so lucky Dan found your Grace. "We're hopeful Wesley will marry a young lady as lovely and gracious." She briefly flicked her hawkish gaze onto him before refocusing on her guests.

Doing his best to hide his anger at his mother's swipe, Wes stepped away from his brother and approached Mr. and Mrs. Adamson. "It's a pleasure to meet you, ma'am." He shook her hand.

Mr. Adamson stepped forward and thrust his hand out. "Harvey Adamson. A pleasure, Wesley." Masculine and jovial, Grace's father grinned wide under the greying moustache. He wore a grey suit complete with a blue and green striped tie that highlighted a build reminiscent of a soccer player. Wes surmised the man must have been quite the lady-killer in his younger years.

Wes grasped the outstretched hand and shook. "Like-wise, sir."

Mrs. Adamson beamed with pride, motioning toward Grace. "This is our son, Clark."

Wes turned to address Grace's brother, and his breath caught in his throat. A stunning, dark-haired man stepped away from Grace and approached. Clark Adamson stood a bit shorter than Wes, but the emerald of his eyes commanded attention. Black-rimmed glasses framed his face, stark against the pale of his skin. *Not pale*, Wes mused. *Just not tanned.* Clark stood in front of Wes, his smile showing off perfect teeth. He stretched out his hand.

GRASPING WES'S HAND, Clark struggled to keep his voice even and took in Dan's brother. Wes had certainly gotten the looks in the family. Though Dan wasn't physically unattractive by any means, Wes far outshined the other Palucinskis. Dark hair, perfectly styled but not pretentious, stunning blue eyes, though not the sapphire of Mitch's, and full lips begging for a kiss, Wes Palucinski brought Mitch's comment from their first meeting to his mind: *You just haven't found the right guy yet.*

The tall, slender man stared right back while shaking Clark's hand, and Clark noticed the contrast between Wes's olive complexion and his own pale skin. He didn't release the grip right away, and Clark started to feel uncomfortable. Mrs. Palucinski narrowed her eyes at their clasped hands.

Clark shook his hand and then eased his grip, a hint that the man should let go. "A pleasure to meet you, Wesley."

Wes cleared his throat. "Likewise."

Extracting his hand, Clark took in the room. The china set out on the table was a pretty pattern, blue with rings of green in the middle and silver around the edges. Ornate silver flatware rested on hunter-green napkins over an antique, lace tablecloth. The wine glasses looked to be crystal.

Looking around the dining room, Clark's mother gushed. "Such a beautiful table setting." She turned to Mrs. Palucinski. "You shouldn't have gone to so much trouble."

"Oh, it's no trouble at all. Sol and I *love* to entertain, and it gives me an opportunity to pull all this out of the china cabinet." She led Clark's mother around the table. "The silver belonged to my grandmother, and the china was a gift from Sol's parents for our wedding."

Turning to Dan's brother, Clark smiled. "Do you

prefer Wesley or Wes? Grace refers to you as Wes."

Wes cleared his throat again. "Yeah, Wes is great."

Hurrying to stand between them, Mrs. Palucinski announced to the room. "Everything is ready if you'd all like to take a seat."

Dan and Grace led Clark's parents to the table. There were ten chairs, so Dan and Grace took two, and his parents took the other two beside them. Wes sat next to the end of the table, and Clark assumed Mr. Palucinski would be on the end.

As he pulled out the chair next to Wes, Mrs. Palucinski interceded. "No, I think it best if you sit over there." She pointed to the opposite side of the table, between Clark's mother and Grace. There was no chair where she indicated.

His mother cocked her head with a furrowed brow, while Clark stared at Grace, wondering what was going on.

Grace's brow also furrowed, but she shrugged.

Mrs. Palucinski laughed, a nervous edge to her voice. "I do think it's important to have everyone in the correct placement."

Clark's parents rose and shifted down, his father, looking quite uncomfortable, taking the end of the table.

Clark glanced at Wes who gave him a shrug and a frown. Stepping around the table, Clark took the seat between his mother and Grace. He had the odd sensation of being the small child out of place and unwelcome at the grown-up's table.

Mr. Palucinski took the head of the table, and, as Mrs. Palucinski strode back into the kitchen, Wes stood and moved down a seat to sit directly across from Clark. When the matriarch of the house returned, Clark caught the scowl she shot her son, before she resumed her hostess smile and placed a large tray in the center of the table. She hurried back into the kitchen.

"So, Clark. I didn't see your name on the list of the guys attending Dan's bachelor party." Wes arched an eyebrow at his brother before continuing. "Are you able to come?"

The absolute last thing Clark wanted to do was attend the bachelor party surrounded by Dan's fraternity brothers. "I hadn't heard about it."

"It's the night before the wedding in Anacortes." Dan gave a slight shake of his head to Wes that Clark caught. His soon-to-be brother-in-law blanched. "I doubt it's your scene, Clark."

Ah. Clark's hands tightened in his lap. That's why he hadn't heard about it. Dan didn't want him there. He had no idea what Grace saw in the man. Now that he had a date to the wedding, albeit a hired date, Clark felt more confident he could handle the evening, *especially* if his presence made Dan uncomfortable. Smiling inwardly, Clark shrugged. "Oh, I don't know. I like alcohol and a room of guys enjoying themselves." Then he gave Dan a fake smile.

Dan scowled until Grace elbowed him in the ribs. He cleared his throat and nodded. "Wes can give you the details."

Mrs. Palucinski came back carrying a salad bowl and a tray of roasted vegetables. "Here we are." After placing them on the table, she lifted the lid off the roast pan. The scent of roasted pork and way too much rosemary quickly filled the room.

Clark's mother patted his leg and turned to their hostess. "It looks divine. Thank you for having us over to dinner."

"Oh, it's our pleasure." Mrs. Palucinski flushed red, taking her seat next to Wes and grasping his hand in hers. "Sol, would you say the blessing?"

With a sideways glance at his sister, Clark took her hand, as well as his mother's, and bowed his head.

Before Mr. Palucinski's voice rumbled across the table, Grace tapped her index finger against Clark's palm. A warning.

Clark braced.

"Lord, bless this table and keep your guiding light bright for the sinners amongst us."

Grace's hand tightly squeezed around Clark's, and she sucked in a breath. Clark winced when her fingernails dug into his palm.

The blessing continued. "May you lead those currently in the darkness of temptation onto the righteous path. Amen."

"Amen," Mrs. Palucinski echoed, her voice clipped and expression dour. Then she lifted the bowl of salad and passed it to her husband.

Clark brought his gaze up to see Wes roll his eyes and turn to address his father. "That seemed a little more *righteous* than normal, Dad."

"It's a message that needs to be heard." The patriarch

of the family shot Clark a quick glance before dishing some of the salad onto his plate.

Clark's eyes widened, and he struggled to accept that Mr. Palucinski had just taken a swipe at him. *What the hell?*

Turning away from his father, Wes addressed Clark's mother. "Grace tells me you play bridge."

A blatant change of subject.

She took the salad bowl from Clark's dad. "Yes, I get together once a week with a group of friends. I know it's terribly old-fashioned of me, but I enjoy it. Gives us girls some time to gossip." She turned to Wes's mother. "You'd be welcome to join us. We meet every Tuesday."

Mrs. Palucinski stiffened but struggled to keep her best-hostess demeanor from slipping. "Thank you, but I don't play cards."

Undeterred, Clark's mother passed the bowl along to Clark. "Well, if you'd ever like to learn, we have a lot of fun."

Clark examined the offering. Iceberg lettuce with barely ripe tomatoes, cucumber, and celery. Not wanting to appear rude, he dutifully dished a small portion of the salad onto his plate. He handed off the salad bowl to Grace.

"I'm sure." Mrs. Palucinski turned her hawkish gaze to Clark. "And what do you do, young man?"

With his mother holding the patter of sliced roast, Clark used his fork to take a piece of the meat and set it on his plate. "I do accounting work for a non-profit focused on helping kids who come from broken homes, and kids forced onto the streets with nowhere else to go." With how uncomfortable the Palucinskis were making him feel, he decided to keep the fact that the kids were LGBTQ out of the conversation.

"I would hope that your employers do thorough background checks." She took a sip from her water glass, her gaze staring down her hawkish nose and holding him in its crosshairs.

Clark ignored his mother's gasp. He peered at her curiously. "It's a matter of course for most accounting professionals."

Her lips pursed. "Well, hopefully, the check was thorough. Gays usually don't get jobs working near impressionable children, do they?"

THE SILENCE IN the room was deafening. Wes sat still for a moment, shock prickling up the small hairs on his arms. Then he shot a gaze filled with daggers at his mother.

But she just smiled sweetly at Grace's family, seemingly unconcerned that the entire Adamson family had gone stone-faced and silent.

Placing his napkin over his barely touched plate, Clark pushed back his chair and rose. "It's been quite an evening, Mr. and Mrs. Palucinski. If you'll excuse me, I'm late for an appointment."

The smile disappeared from Wes's mother's face. "Oh?"

His expression as hard as marble, Clark shot a glare at the two hosts and strode from the room.

Wes assessed the rest of the table. His mother glanced at his father, a half-smile on her lips.

Grace looked like she might combust, face bright red, brows knitted, and gaze narrowed at Dan.

His brother wilted under the intensity of his fiancée's fury. "Um, Mom, that was uncalled for."

Wes could tell his brother's admonishment was less than half-hearted.

The Adamsons just stared at each other.

Pushing back his own chair, Wes stood. "I'll see him out." Before his mother could say anything, Wes stalked from the dining room and hurried down the hallway to the front door.

Standing in the entryway, Clark was slipping his arms into his coat. He glanced up at Wes with a frown and shrugged his shoulders into the jacket.

"Clark, wait." Wes stepped next to him.

"Why?" His gaze didn't meet Wes's. He pulled his cell from his pocket.

"I'm absolutely mortified by my mother's behavior. I'm so sorry she insulted you." Wes stared at the floor.

"Your father got in a good swipe, too. Though I appreciate your apology, I'm ordering a car. No need to stay where I'm not welcome." He stared at the phone for a moment.

Not feeling terribly welcome himself, Wes was about to offer Clark a ride when a voice carried down the hallway.

"No need, sweetheart." Clark's mother led the way into the entryway with a pleasant but determined smile, followed closely by a scowling Mr. Adamson. "We'll give you a ride home."

Wes's mother scurried behind them. "Oh, please don't go. I have a lovely dessert."

Fuck, his mother was clueless.

Mrs. Adamson ignored her, and instead addressed Wes. "Would you be a dear and get our coats, Wesley?"

"Right away, Mrs. Adamson." Wes turned and opened the hall closet. He grabbed both of their coats, and his own, holding open Mrs. Adamson's for her. "May I help you on with your coat?"

"Thank you, Wesley. That's very gentlemanly of you." Mrs. Adamson stepped into the coat, and Wes let go.

He turned to Mr. Adamson and held out his coat. "Sir?"

A curt "thank you" was all the man could muster. From the reddening of his face and the trembling of his hands, Wes hoped Clark and Mrs. Adamson would be able to calm him in the car. From his increasing fury, Wes feared the poor guy might have a heart attack or an aneurism.

Wes held open the door for the Adamsons and stepped in front of his mother, blocking her from the departing guests. "I'm so sorry for the insulting behavior you've had to endure."

Mrs. Adamson paused and patted his cheek. "You're a very sweet young man." She eyed him appraisingly, and he felt some discomfort under her gaze. After a glance at Clark, she turned back to him. "I hope we'll see more of you, Wesley."

Turning on her heel, she didn't say another word to Wes's mother, who sulked in the hallway with her arms crossed. Clark and Mr. Adamson followed out the door.

Wes closed it behind them. Taking a deep breath, he rounded on his mother. "Satisfied?"

"I don't know what upset him so much." She waved a hand in the air. "Some people are overly sensitive."

Slipping into his own coat, Wes leveled an angry glare at her. "You knew damned well what you were doing."

Her eyes widened as her lips pursed. "Wesley! Language."

Without another word, Wes pulled open the door to see the taillights of the Adamson's car speed away.

"Wesley, come back here this instant!"

His mother's shrill command grated on his ears. He slammed the door behind him so hard, the glass of the window next to the frame shook. Not looking back, he stalked down the drive to the sidewalk.

The cool air did nothing to calm his temper. Clark had been nothing but polite and sweet, and in return, he'd been treated horrifically by Wes's family—because he was gay. Shaking his head, Wes walked the block to his car. He realized he could never come out to his parents. And that stupid brother of his had done nothing to stick up for his fiancée's brother. *I hope she dumps him.*

Considering the dinner debacle, Wes decided an evening alone wasn't something he wanted. He pulled out his phone and called the guy he kept on speed dial for just such an emergency.

After two rings, a deep voice answered. "Wesley,

how're you doing?"

"Not great. Have some time this evening?" He crossed his fingers.

"The family?" The deep, comforting voice calmed his fury somewhat.

Wes sighed. "Yeah. The dinner with my brother's fiancée and her family was a disaster."

"Sorry to hear that. I'm free in about an hour. Want me to come to your place?"

"Sure." He reached his car and leaned against the frame. "I'll grab a quick bite and meet you there."

"Didn't you have dinner?"

"About three bites before my mother attacked the very sweet and really hot gay brother of my future sister-in-law." He pictured Clark sitting there with his dumbstruck expression before the hurt and insult took over.

"How about I meet you at that pub you like so much?"

Wes puffed out a breath. "You know, that sounds great."

"See you shortly. Get a beer, and I'll relax you after dinner."

Wes's cock stirred. Knowing what his friend had in mind, Wes couldn't wait to get on his back. He ended the call and pocketed his cell.

Snorting as he unlocked his car, he tugged open the door and slipped behind the driver's seat. *If Grace still wants to marry Dan, next weekend is going to be a nightmare.*

Chapter Four

"ARE YOU KIDDING me with this?" Roger Matthews asked, his beer poised at his lips.

"Serious as a fucking heart attack," Clark fumed. "Which is about what my Dad had." He took a gulp of his beer, grateful to find his best friend at their usual pub.

Since the big blow up had smoothed over between Jason and Roger, Clark found himself frequenting the quaint pub in the Ravenna neighborhood more and more. The Australian meat-and-cheese pies and tater tots had found another convert, though Clark mused he hardly needed all the fried food and calories before Grace's wedding. On the other hand, after that dinner party, there might not be a wedding.

A roar went up from the pool table in the corner, and Clark glanced over to see Roger's partner, SPD Officer Paul Tomlinson, raising a pool stick in triumph.

Officer Jason Lynch swaggered over to the table, a wide grin on his face. "Hey, guys. Looks like Paul ran the table. Mike's been working with him."

Sure enough, Jason's husband, Mike Bryant, stood patting Paul on the back and pointing at the table with his other hand. Clark remembered Roger talking about the couple, Alex and Sarah Templeton, who stood holding their pool cues and shaking their heads. They gazed forlornly at the table while the other police officer, Fred something-or-other, beamed his happiness.

Jason grabbed the third chair at the table. "How's the kid I dropped off working out?"

Not thrilled at the intrusion, Clark sighed and turned to Jason. "Fine. He's interested in numbers and accounting. I'm thinking we can get him into a program at the community college to get him started." Clark had to keep reminding himself that Roger had forgiven Jason for the bullshit things he'd insinuated in this very pub, and the cop had been true to his word on trying to make it up to Roger and Paul.

"Great," Jason said with a good-natured grin. "What were you guys talking about?"

Roger piped up before Clark could say anything. "Clark was just telling me about a really shitty dinner with his sister's future in-laws this evening. Homophobes, by the sound of it."

The grin disappeared. "What did they do to you?" Jason's brow furrowed.

The intensity and seriousness of his stare and question surprised Clark. "Uh, Dan's mother asked why the House let a gay accountant anywhere near *impressionable kids.*" He air-quoted the last two words.

Jason drew back in his chair, a snarl forming on his lip. "What the hell?"

"That's what I wanted to know," Roger said, throwing his hands up. "If they had any idea all the good that Clark and the foundation do, they'd be embarrassed by what they said."

"Hardly," Clark snorted. "They'd probably ask why those kids weren't sent to conversion therapy or something." He scowled, remembering the prayer Mr. Palucinski had said before they passed the food around.

Jason leaned forward. "Do you know their full names? I could run a background check on them and see if there's something we can bust them on."

A loud laugh rang out, and the three of them turned toward the laughter. Paul and Mike approached the table, their faces alight with amusement.

Paul glanced at each of them, his smile dropping to a worried frown. "Everyone getting along?" He eyed Jason. "Did you say something to upset my fiancé?"

"No!" Jason looked from Roger to Clark. "Back me up, guys."

Clark exchanged a quick glance and a wink with Roger, and then turned to Paul. "He said some terrible things about my sister's in-laws."

Face whitening, Jason swung his gaze at Paul. "No, I just wanted to see if they had any outstanding charges, swear."

"You want to arrest them," Clark stated sadly, staring at the table and shaking his head. "And after what I told you they said about me."

"Damn it, Lynch!" Paul thundered.

Clark widened his eyes. Though startled by Paul's outburst, seeing Jason squirm made the joke worthwhile.

Mike rolled his eyes. "Shit, Jason. We talked about

this."

"But, I didn't...I mean, yeah, but..." Jason spluttered.

Roaring with laughter, Roger patted Clark's shoulder. "You're terrible."

Paul and Mike shared a glance, and then turned their narrowing gazes on Clark.

Unable to still his chuckles, Clark broke into a grin. "My sister's future in-laws said some really homophobic shit about me. Jason, here, is ready to run them in on any technicality he can find."

Paul straddled the chair next to Clark. "You know, you're a shit sometimes."

Snagging a chair from the next table, Mike settled in beside to his husband. "Sorry, baby. I shouldn't have doubted you." He kissed Jason's cheek.

Jason crossed his arms in front of his chest with a scowl. "See if I ever offer to help you again, Clark."

The buzzing in his pocket distracted Clark, and he fished the phone out of his pocket. Grace's laughing face filled the screen. He glanced up. "It's my sister. This should be good." He accepted the call. Before she said a word, he shook his head. "I don't even want to hear it, Grace."

"Oh my God, Clark," she fumed. "I can't believe that happened to you."

He puffed out a breath. "You aren't the only one." The four other guys hung on his every word. "I'm going to take this outside." He pushed back his chair and stood, hurrying to the door.

"Clark, are you still there?" his sister's worried voice

asked.

"Yeah, hold on until I get outside. I'm at a pub and it's loud in here." He furrowed his brow. "I didn't get dinner, remember?"

"Shit," she said.

Reaching the exit, he pushed open the door. The din of the bar faded when he stepped into the cold, night air. "Okay, go ahead."

"I know you're probably done with Dan–" she began.

He barked a laugh. "Damned right, I am. Worthless piece of shit. Why the hell are you marrying him again?"

"I love him." Clark opened his mouth to speak, but she cut him off. "Before you say anything else, let me explain."

"Explain what?" Clark exploded. "How you're marrying a fucking homophobe and making his evil parents part of our family?"

"I know, Clark," she replied, her voice sharp. "Okay? He tried to intercede—"

"That was the most half-hearted defense I've ever heard." He paused, trying to compose himself. "I can't believe the girl who defended me all through high school is marrying someone like that. It makes me sick to my stomach, Grace."

She sighed heavily. "I was afraid you'd go there. Look, Clark. I read them all the riot act after you left. Wes walked out, too. Dan apologized to me and begged me not to cancel the wedding."

"And what's going to be different?" Clark fumed. "He'll get you to marry him, and then act worse once he gets a ring on your finger."

"I'm working on him. I swear, if he does one more thing to you, I'll call it all off, but I want to give him the last chance he's asking for. I've already told him I'll divorce him if he tries anything after we're married."

Clark shook his head, disgust welling up in his gut. "I can't fucking believe you're still even entertaining the idea of marrying that piece of shit."

"Please, Clark. For me. Just give him another chance. I promise it'll be different next time you see him." Her voice hardened. "And if it's not, he's history."

Leaning against the cool bricks of the building, Clark closed his eyes. The last thing he wanted was to give Dan Palucinski another chance to insult him, let alone get anywhere near the man's vile family. At least Dan's brother had the decency to apologize. His mind wandered back to that lingering handshake, Wes's firm grip but soft hands.

"Clark?"

Grace's voice broke his reverie, and he straightened. "Okay, Grace. One more chance. But if anything happens at your wedding, I'm out, and as long as you're with him, we're done. Got it?"

"Loud and clear. Thanks, Clark. I wish you could see him like I do."

"So. Do. I," Clark grumbled.

"WHAT DO YOU want, Dan?" Wes snapped into the phone. Though he'd been able to blow off some steam the prior evening after he stormed out of his parents' house,

Wes had been fuming all morning. The unwelcomed phone call from his brother did nothing to improve his mood.

"What's your problem, bro?" Dan asked, irritation coloring his tone. "Mom's really upset with you."

Wes sprang up from his desk and slammed his office door. "I don't fucking care. If Grace is stupid enough to still want to marry you, get one of your asshole frat buddies to be your best man. I'm not going anywhere near Anacortes this weekend."

"Oh, come on, Wes. Why are you getting all wound up because mom laid into that little fag?"

"Do you even hear yourself?" Wes roared into his cell. "Our parents were incredibly and unforgivably rude to Clark and the Adamsons."

"Shit," Dan muttered. "Grace said you'd be mad, but I didn't believe her."

"You better believe I'm angry." Wes sat back at his desk, glaring at the wooden surface and trying to get his temper under control. Though he adored Grace, he'd had enough from his family for a good long time. The thought of spending an entire weekend with them made his stomach churn.

"Grace was, too. I've never see her so angry. She ripped Mom and Dad apart."

Wes massaged his right temple with his thumb and middle finger. "And what did she say to you?"

"She told me if I mess up one more time, we're through."

Shifting the phone to his other ear, Wes grabbed the

mouse sitting next to his monitor and woke up his computer. "So, if I call Grace right now and say you wanted to know why I'm so worked up over how her 'fag' brother was treated, she'd dump your ass?"

"Fuck, Wes." Fear crept into Dan's voice. "I'm your brother, man. Don't do that to me. I really love Grace."

"Nice to know you give a shit about someone," Wes muttered. He clicked open the ad campaign he and Emily had been working on. "What exactly do you want from me, Dan? Apparently, unlike you, I'm actually working today."

"Just say that you'll still be my best man."

The worry and pleading in Dan's voice gave Wes pause. He stared at his screen, the brilliant colors of the storyboards displayed across his monitor. If he went to the wedding, he might have another chance to talk to Clark. Wes envied the man for being out and having the full support of his family, and he found himself wanting to get to know his future brother-in-law.

"Still there, bro?" Dan's voice shook. "I need you there."

"Okay, Dan," Wes said, pushing away from his screen and staring back at his office door. "I'll give you the same deal you got from Grace. I'll be there and do all the best man things. But if you fuck up, Grace isn't the only one done with you." The other end of the phone went quiet. After a moment, Wes grew impatient. "Yes or no, Dan?"

"Okay, bro. Thanks."

"Good. I have to get back to work. I'm putting in extra hours so I can take Friday off." He didn't give Dan a chance to respond. His brother didn't need to know Emily was giving him extra time off.

He ended the call and immediately powered off his phone, dreading the rest of the week and his mother's wrath at slamming the door in her face. Though Emily had insisted on him taking this week off, Wes had stormed into the office that morning, needing work to keep his mind off the prior evening's debacle.

Next week. I'll take next week off.

BRIGHT AND EARLY Wednesday morning, Clark sat in a small coffee shop a couple blocks from the House, drumming his fingers on the table. His Americano steamed in front of him, but he continued to stare out the window. Should he call Mitch and warn him? Maybe just call the whole arrangement off and not go to the wedding? He smiled wryly at the thought of not having to deal with Dan or the Palucinskis. Grace would kill him for not showing, but he'd bet she'd get it.

But then, there was dreamy Wes with the lingering handshake. The one good thing from Grace's upcoming marriage was meeting and spending some time with Dan's brother. He was amazed two such different men came from the same parents.

The bell over the door to the coffee shop jingled, and Clark jolted at the sight of Wes steeping inside, almost like he'd conjured him. Wes froze and stared at Clark until the slowly closing door bumped his ass.

Clark chuckled at the red creeping up Wes's neck and

across his face. With a wave, Clark stood and pulled out the chair across from his seat. "Join me?"

With a nod, Wes gave a sleepy grin. "Let me grab a coffee. I'm barely awake." He shuffled to the counter and ordered while Clark sat back down.

Wes seemed to be comfortable in his skin, not bothered in the slightest by his sister-in-law's gay brother. Raking his gaze over the other man, Clark appreciated the broad shoulders, the well-defined vee of his back, and his pert ass.

Grabbing the coffee from the barista, Wes turned and joined Clark at his table. "Hey, glad I ran into you."

"Likewise. Do you live around here?" Clark asked.

Wes shook his head. "I have an appointment with my doctor this morning, so I thought I'd walk around the neighborhood and grab a coffee. How about you?"

"I work about a block and a half away. I'm with the Firestone House doing their accounting." He frowned, eyeing Wes. "I passed my background check, by the way."

Blanching, Wes stared at Clark. "I can't tell you enough how embarrassed and sorry I am for my parents' behavior. Both were completely out of line." Glancing away, he took a sip of his coffee.

Not quite willing to let the subject go, Clark kept his gaze firmly fixed on Wes. "And what about you?" Though he got the idea Dan's brother didn't think the same as the rest of his family, he needed to hear it from Wes's own lips.

Meeting Clark's stare, Wes showed no sign of hesitation. "I don't subscribe to the crap peddled by them or their preacher, much to my mother's dismay."

Clark relaxed. "That's good to hear. Mom gushed about how sweet she thought you were."

Another blush crept up Wes's neck. "Nice of her to say." Wes scrunched his forehead, seeming to be on the verge of saying something further, but he gave a little shake of his head and took another swig of his coffee.

They sat together in silence for a few minutes, each working on their coffees and staring out the window. Finally, Clark returned his gaze to Wes. "I'm thinking about not going to the wedding."

Wes jerked his head to stare at Clark, eyes wide with alarm. "Oh, no. Please come. I'll keep my parents away from you."

"I don't think I want to subject my date to Dan." Clark thought of the hunky Mitch. The man likely dealt with all kinds of people and prejudices in his line of work, and he could probably handle the Palucinskis just fine.

A cloud shadowed Wes's face for a moment, but it passed quickly, and he smiled. "Just think how freaked out my folks'll be when you have some guy hanging off you at their son's wedding. I'd actually like to see that."

Clark shrugged, a grin inching across his own lips. "Might be fun. Grace did threaten Dan to be nice to me."

Wes's lips tightened. "I told him, one more fuck-up and I'm done with him, too."

"You did?" Clark could hardly believe Wes would willingly walk away from his own brother.

"This has been a long time coming." Wes frowned. "I don't want to burden you with the details, but I'm sick of his bullshit. If he wants to be a carbon copy of our parents, I don't need to be around him."

"Wow," Clark breathed. He couldn't imagine a situation that would make him completely turn his back on Grace, although the whole Dan situation made him wonder how he'd continue a relationship with her. But then, his family tended to talk through issues and stayed close. Sometimes too close, but always surrounding each other with love.

"Anyway…" Wes stood. "I need to get going." He stuck out his hand.

Clark rose and shook, enjoying the warmth of the other man's hand. "I'm glad we ran into each other."

Not letting go, Wes stared into Clark's eyes. "I am, too." They stood together for a moment, still touching, but then Wes shook his head. "Sorry." He let go and grabbed his cup from the table. "I'll see you Friday in Anacortes?"

Nodding, Clark snagged his empty cup and saucer, the heat of their connection leaving him a little confused. "I'll see you there."

CHAPTER FIVE

TWO DAYS LATER, Wes buzzed with irritation. Dan had dumped quite a bit of the wedding prep on his shoulders, though Wes chose not to take Thursday off work after all. Friday had come too quickly. Wes held his cell to his ear and tossed underwear into his overnight bag. "Yes, Dan, I got them. Don't worry. I have a list of everything I'm supposed to bring."

"Okay, bro. Did you grab the cigars?"

Wes wrinkled his nose in anticipation of the acrid smoke. "Unfortunately. Those things are disgusting. Why do you want to smoke them at your bachelor party?"

"Celebration, man." His voice vibrated with excitement. "I got a hot girl to marry me. Why wouldn't I celebrate?"

"I thought you'd left the frat house." Shaking his head, he picked up a pen and checked off the box next to the word *underwear* on his To Bring list.

"Okay, bro. Most important. Did you score a chick for the wedding?"

With a sigh, Wes turned away from his dresser and sat on the chair next to his bed. "That's not an item on my list," he replied frostily, hoping Dan would get the hint to drop the subject.

"Dude! You still don't have a date?"

Clueless asshole. His brother's voice rose, and Wes held the phone away from his ear as he rolled his eyes.

Irritated at the delay to his schedule and at having to hash this subject out again, he huffed. "No, I don't."

"Geez," Dan groaned. "What about Veronica?"

"Busy. So are Miah, Celeste, and Taylor." He hadn't actually checked with any of the girls he'd mentioned to his brother as possibilities. Two of them didn't even exist, and Taylor was a hot little twink he'd had a one-nighter with about four months ago. "I tried to get someone, but no one's available." He chuckled, sure that his mother would completely lose it if Wes brought a guy as his date. Clark bringing one was sure to get under her skin, and he relished seeing his prim and proper family uptight around the gay couple, especially after their behavior the other night.

"That's okay, bro," Dan said, the unmistakable tone of pity in his voice. "Grace has some hot friends from her sorority coming. You can probably hook up with one of them."

Shaking his head, Wes stood and stepped to the closet. "Okay, gotta go. If you want me there before the welcome reception starts, I need to finish packing and get on the road."

"Wes…"

Something in his brother's tone made Wes pause.

"You need to find a girl to settle down with. You're already over thirty."

Dan's tone was serious—something Wes hadn't heard from his brother in a long time. Wes regretted that he couldn't be truthful with his only sibling. Injecting humor into his voice to deflect, he said, "You're almost there, you little shit." He slid the door open and checked his tux. "My lack of relationship isn't something you need to concern yourself with."

His brother's voice shifted to a worried tone. "Bro, I'm just afraid you're not going to find anyone to marry."

Turning around to face the dresser again, Wes sighed. In these moments, he wanted to come out to Dan, but he knew full well how his brother and parents felt. "You concentrate on your marriage and let me worry about my love life. Who says I don't have contingencies?"

His mind drifted to the guy he'd been paying to see every couple of weeks. Rippling muscles and red hair, the escort excited Wes to no end, but Wes made sure to keep feelings and sex separate. After that horrible dinner, Wes had run to Mitch's arms and poured out his troubles. The next morning, he'd woken up in the escort's arms, feeling secure and safe. A relationship would be nice, but until he could be out and free to live as he wished, he found paying for a service easier, safer, and more private than trying to find a discreet guy who wasn't married. He'd been able to face the week, but worried that the nagging attraction he felt toward Mitch was due to more than the man's muscles. Maybe the impending wedding was fucking with his head, because he could see how lucky his brother was that Grace still wanted to marry him.

"Well, okay, bro," Dan said, doubt in his voice. "I'll

let you go. Don't forget to call Mom and Dad before you leave."

Wes cringed. Since the dinner, he'd avoided his parents, especially his mother. Still, he knew he'd have to face the music with her eventually. He'd better get it over with before they all showed up in Anacortes, pretending to be a happy family.

"Oh, one last thing," his brother said. "Remind me to behave myself if I get out of line around Clark—you know, Grace's gay brother."

A flush of heat spread over Wes's cheeks as he envisioned the bright smile of Dan's future brother-in-law. "Really? And why would you need my help with that?"

"Grace made it clear I have to be nice to him," Dan grumbled. "And so did you."

"It's not difficult, Dan," he retorted, irritation mounting again. "How about you treat him like everyone else? You know, like a human being."

"Yeah, but dude, he's one of those *fags*." Dan sounded like he was describing an embarrassing disease.

Jesus. Wes closed his eyes and willed himself to keep calm. Each time his brother spoke of Clark, or of any other gay person, he had to use the f-word. "Dan, you're being a dick. Clark is a nice guy. You'd know that if you spent five minutes speaking to him with an open mind. I had a great conversation with him a couple mornings ago."

The other end of the call went silent for a moment.

"Dan?" He checked the screen of his cell, seeing the call still connected and the seconds ticking on the call time.

"Why did you hook up with him?" Dan's tone weighed low and suspicious.

"I ran into him at a coffee shop on Capital Hill." Wes chuckled. "We discussed not going to your Anacortes love fest."

"He's not coming?" Dan's voice held an annoying amount of hope.

"Oh, he's coming," Wes said, drawing out the moment. "And he's bringing a date." A twinge of disappointment hit Wes, not only that Clark was bringing a guy, but that Wes had no chance of being that guy.

"Fuck," Dan huffed. "Did he make a pass at you? At least you were somewhere public."

Wes's annoyance flared. "You know, Dan, you're damned lucky he hasn't talked Grace out of marrying your sorry ass."

"But…"

Finally at the end of his rope with his brother, he cut Dan off before he said something he'd regret. "I'm out. See you in Anacortes." He ended the call. After making sure his phone was off, he threw it onto the bed. *Asshole. That's why I don't come out to you.*

CLARK PULLED UP to one of the new condo buildings situated along Fifteenth Avenue Northwest. The five-story building had once been a couple of quaint houses and a coffee shop. Now, a large Italian restaurant filled the bottom floor, and glass and brick rose above the eatery. He sent a quick text to Mitch and tapped his steering wheel while he waited. His thoughts swirled at the events of the last week—the new kid at the shelter, the dinner at the Palucinskis, running into Wes in the coffee shop, and the long days balancing the accounts for the auditors.

Tanner came to the top of the maelstrom, and he considered how he could help the kid. College for sure. Clark continued to be grateful for the huge donation from the man the non-profit was named after. Several other donors had signed on after the initial gift, and the college fund endowment paid for all the kids' educations just from the dividends on the investments.

His companion emerged from the front door of the condos, and Clark pushed work from his mind. After this weekend, he'd have plenty of time to decide on the best course of action for Tanner.

Approaching the car, Mitch waved. A black jacket barely contained his chest and hung open to reveal a forest green button-up shirt. Gray slacks hugged his muscular legs and fit perfectly over the contours of his butt.

He opened the car door. "Hey, handsome." Mitch's gaze raked over him. "Wow."

Clark gave a slight shake of his head. "Thanks, though I think I'm more nervous than handsome."

With a chuckle, Mitch hopped into the car, tossed his bag in the back seat, and slammed the door shut. "Both, actually. Don't be nervous. No glasses?"

"Nah, contacts this weekend. I don't like the glasses in pictures."

"I think they look hot on you." He leaned in and brushed his lips against Clark's. "We're going to have a great weekend."

"That remains to be seen, though if it's not good, I'll definitely hear about it." He envisioned Grace and remembered their conversation about Dan after that horrible dinner. Shifting the car into gear, he pulled out into traffic. "My sister warned lover-boy to be civil."

Mitch arched an eyebrow. "How about you fill me in on all the players at this wedding. Anything I should watch out for?"

"There are *endless* possibilities for drama." Clark chuckled. "It's actually a perfect storm of potential."

"Sounds interesting," Mitch said with a grin. "Let's start with the bride's side and work our way across the aisle."

"Most of the extended family can't come, so it'll be my mother Kathryn, my father Harvey, a couple of cousins, Dad's sister, and of course, my sister Grace." Each person's face came to mind as he listed them off. "Aunt Claire is awesome but very outspoken. Her two sons, Duncan and Leif, are both firemen."

"Whoa," Mitch hummed. "Sexy."

Clark laughed. "And both are very straight. They're awesome, though."

"And you're uncle?"

He shook his head as he merged onto Interstate 5. "Uncle Tony died about five years ago. Heart attack."

"Sorry about that. Were you close to him?"

"Not so much, but my mom adored him." Merging into traffic and then into the carpool lane, he set the cruise control. "He was good to me, but we barely saw him because he worked all the time. Probably why he had the heart attack."

"Okay, so the Widow Claire is awesome with her two studly firemen sons." He held up one hand and counted on his fingers. "Who else?"

"My dad is a mechanical engineer. He'll likely ask a lot of questions." Glancing at his companion, his mind turned to their cover story. "What should we say about how we met and what you do? Both will likely come up."

Mitch grinned. "Don't worry. We can say we met at a coffee shop, and I have an engineering degree from the University of Illinois, so I can hold my own with your dad."

With a start, he swung his gaze from the road to stare at Mitch. "You have an engineering degree? Why are you escorting?"

Laughing, Mitch nodded toward the windshield. "Turn those beautiful eyes back onto the road." He rubbed a beefy hand over Clark's leg.

Clark turned his attention back to driving, trying to ignore the heat transmitting from the warm hand to his crotch. "Sorry, I'm just surprised. Wouldn't you make a lot more in an engineering position?"

With a shrug, Mitch stared out the front window. "Maybe, but I'm not quite ready to settle into a desk job. Escorting gives me a lot of contact with people, and a lot of flexibility with my schedule. It more than adequately pays my bills."

Clark shook his head. "You're full of surprises."

Smirking, Mitch squeezed his thigh. "You have no

idea. Back to the cast of characters."

"Oh, yeah," Clark said, mentally going down the list of his family. "Mom has her bridge club, and she plays twice a week while Dad's at work."

"Seriously?" Mitch asked, his brows raised. "She can't be that old."

With a laugh, he imagined his mother in pearls and a cocktail dress, sporting a beehive hairdo, a highball in front of her, and a cigarette wedged between two fingers while she contemplated her cards. The image definitely didn't suit her.

Mitch cocked an eyebrow. "What?"

"Since Grace and I graduated from high school, she does volunteer work the rest of the week. She likes to keep up with her friends, though, and for God knows what reason, they all decided to play bridge. When they get together, the hens tend to cluck about anything and everything."

Mitch's hand continued rubbing Clark's leg, moving closer to his crotch and dipping along the inside of his thigh. The touch sent light tingles up and down his leg.

"Should be easy enough to schmooze them." He counted off two more fingers. "And your sister?"

His concentration wavered at Mitch's touch. "She's pretty amazing. Pushed me out of the closet when I was sixteen and ruthlessly defended me against the high school bully." Clark chuckled. "She had him crying in front of his gang and ended his reign of terror. No one messed with me after that."

Mitch let out a whistle. "That sounds like a story."

The memory flashed across his mind. "She'd been taking karate classes in the evenings, and he pushed her one too many times. She broke his nose and humiliated him."

"That ended his reign of terror?"

A smirk of satisfaction inched across Clark's lips. "He was stupid enough to try to take her down a second time, and a well-placed kick had him walking funny for over a week. That's when he started bawling his head off. All his thug buddies laughed at him. To top it all off, he got suspended and nothing happened to Grace."

"Nice," Mitch said with a grin then furrowed his brow. "So, if she's such a badass, what's the issue with the groom?"

Clark's stomach soured. "Dan. Daniel Palucinski."

Mitch snorted. "That's a mouthful."

"To put it bluntly, he hates gays. Not entirely his fault. The parents are real pieces of work, especially his mother. Some of those ultra-holy folks." His mind flashed to meeting the Palucinskis and the insults they heaped on him. "Dan is definitely marrying into our family, not vice-versa. He has a really cool brother, though."

"So, the parents are homophobic like Dan?" The corners of Mitch's mouth turned down into a small frown.

"Big time," Clark confirmed. "Those are all of the major players."

"Sounds like an interesting mix." He turned to stare out of the window again while they drove through the city of Everett. "Palucinski... I wonder..." A small smile crept along Mitch's lips.

"What?" Clark changed lanes to pass a slow-moving semi and then glanced at Mitch.

He shook his head, but he stared out the window thoughtfully. "Nothing."

"Geez, bro, what took you so long?" Dan tapped his foot as Wes entered their hotel room. "Grace is gonna freak out that we aren't already at the reception hall."

Pushing his way through the door and balancing a large box in one hand, a bag over one shoulder, and his tuxedo in a garment bag over his other shoulder, Wes glared at his brother. "Really? *Really!* Between the long conversation with Mom about Grace's family, and the long list of crap you needed me to pick up? And *then* the traffic to get up here?"

"Okay, okay." Dan stepped forward and took the box. "Sorry. I appreciate everything you've done."

"I knew you could be a nice guy if you tried." Wes hung the garment bag with his tux in the closet and dropped his overnight bag on the floor.

"I'm on my best behavior for Grace's gay brother." Dan dug through the box and lifted out the cigars.

Fighting his temper, Wes turned to face Dan. "And then you had to go and ruin it. If I were you, I'd avoid the words *gay* and *fag* for the duration of the weekend. His name is Clark. Burn that into your brain. Like I told you on the phone, he's cool." Wes narrowed his gaze. "And I'm reminding you of my warning."

"Bro, chill out," Dan blustered. His mouth pursed like

he'd sucked on a lemon. "It's like you're in love with him or something."

Heat rose in Wes's face. "I'm just looking out for you. Grace isn't going to put up with you dissing her baby brother."

"I know, and I'm trying. That's why I need you to keep me in line." Dan moved over to him and clasped his shoulder. "Can't have her dumping me so close to the wedding."

Trying not to think about Grace's brother, Wes leveled a glare at Dan. "She'll dump you after the wedding just as quickly if you don't stop with your bullshit."

"I'm trying, man," Dan whined. "I'm just a little creeped out by the fa—uh, by Clark."

Wes shook off Dan's hand and dug in his bag for his purple, button-up dress shirt. "You know, I grew up with Mom and Dad's nastiness toward anyone not in their church, and I didn't turn out like you."

Frowning, Dan took a step back. "Aw, come on, man. I'm not that bad."

"No, you're not." Wes lifted the shirt out of the bag. "For some strange reason, you're only a jerk to gay people. It's amazing how nice and respectful you are to everyone else."

"Well, you and Grace can help me with that." A cocky grin spread across Dan's lips.

Lifting the T-shirt over his head, Wes dropped it by his bag and slipped his arms into the sleeves of his purple shirt. "You have to *want* to change, but, so far, I've seen no sign of that."

Dan frowned then glanced at his watch. "Dude, button up and let's get going. We're late."

Grinding his teeth, Wes fastened the buttons and tucked in his shirt. He grabbed his blazer and bowtie from the bag in the closet. "Don't think we're done with this conversation."

CHAPTER SIX

S TEPPING INTO THE reception hall, Clark fought a surge of anxiety. Green and silver streamers hung from the ceiling and circled the room, which teemed with family and friends. Clark spied his sister and his soon-to-be brother-in-law laughing with a group he recognized as her college sorority sisters. Wes hovered at Grace's other side.

Grace glanced his way, and her face lit up. As she waved, Wes turned toward them. He grinned at Clark, but his face stiffened for a brief moment when he spied Mitch. Curious about his reaction, Clark watched the handsome man recover his smile and return to the conversation with the small group surrounding the happy couple.

With a glance at his date, Clark wondered what had caused the momentary reaction, but quickly dismissed it as Grace, Dan, and Wes made an abrupt departure from the gaggle of blonde women and crossed the crowded room.

"Hey, baby brother. How are you?" Grace threw her arms around Clark.

Clark gave her a squeeze. "Doing well." He pulled away and shook Dan's hand. "Hi, Dan."

"Hey, Clark. Glad you made it." Friendly, yet frosty and stiff at the same time, his future brother-in-law's reception didn't make him feel all that welcome. Though Dan's reception was less blatantly averse than his parents', Clark got the impression Dan still wasn't terribly comfortable around "the gay brother" despite Grace's threats.

Surveying Clark's date, a wry smile curved Grace's lips. "And who is this?"

With a step back, Clark settled a hand on Mitch's shoulder. "Grace, Dan, Wes, this is Mitch."

"Nice to meet you." Grace extended her hand.

Mitch grasped her fingers and kissed the back of her hand. "A pleasure. Congratulations on your upcoming nuptials. Dan, here, is a lucky man."

She giggled as Mitch released her hand and clasped Dan's. Stifling a laugh, Clark watched Dan stiffen while he shook hands with Mitch. Somewhere between a glower and a wince, his sister's fiancé quickly extracted his hand and nodded.

Finally, Mitch turned to Wes, extending his hand once again. "Nice to meet you."

Wes's forced smile faltered again, matching his brother's wince under Mitch's grip. "Likewise."

Clark saw something pass between Wes and Mitch, and their hands stayed clasped for an uncomfortable moment. If Clark had to assign an emotion, he'd think the expression Wes displayed in his suddenly pinched features was fear.

Seeming to realize he was still holding Mitch's hand, Wes released it and stepped backward. He turned to Clark. "I'm glad to see you decided to come after that nightmare of a dinner with my parents."

Dan's frown deepened. "It wasn't a *disaster*, Wes."

"You weren't the focus of Mom's nastiness," Wes crisply replied.

A hard stare passed between the brothers.

Clark rolled his eyes at Dan's comment. "Don't worry, Dan." The brothers returned their attention to him. "It was definitely a one-time thing. Your mom and I don't need to be anywhere near each other after tomorrow."

Grace cleared her throat and hiked an eyebrow at her fiancé. Dan grimaced and tugged at the collar of his shirt, much to Clark's amusement. Grace, as usual, had Dan by the balls.

Chuckling, Wes patted Clark's shoulder. "Well, on that happy note…"

Grace's hand shot up, and she waved to a thin, bespectacled guy next to the entrance. "Randy!" Hooking her arms around Dan's and Wes's elbows, she pulled the two men away. "Sorry, Clark, we have to run. That's the reverend, and we need to discuss some things with him before the rehearsal."

Raising an eyebrow, Clark tried not to laugh outright. "Your minister's name is *Randy*?"

She rolled her eyes. "Now we *definitely* need to run. Don't forget to say hi to Aunt Claire."

"No worries. We'll have plenty of time to catch up." Clark chuckled at the retreating trio and turned to his date. "I don't think Dan was expecting you to be so strong, and Wes is just acting weird."

Staring at the groom's brother, Mitch shook his head

but said nothing. The same smile he'd seen in the car curved Mitch's lips.

Before Clark could pursue the subject further, he spied the familiar gray bun of Aunt Claire. His two cousins flanked her like a pair of firefighter bodyguards.

She strode with purpose toward him, a warm smile spreading across her lips. "Clark, sweetheart. Give your Aunt Claire a hug." She held out her arms.

Without hesitation, Clark enveloped her, smelling the faint apple scent of her signature soap. He'd grown up with that smell, visiting her when he was a kid. With a glance at his cousin Duncan, Clark hugged her tighter and lifted her off the ground. "I'm so happy to see you."

"Clark!" she squawked.

Duncan laughed. "Put her down, cuz. She's old and fragile."

"Oooh!" Aunt Claire smacked Clark's arm then rounded on her son. "Duncan Adam Ramsey, I'll have you know I'm in the prime of my life."

Rolling his eyes, Duncan turned to his brother. "Sure, Mom. But well past half-time."

Leif laughed and reached out to shove his brother.

"You just wait, Tweedledee and Tweedledum," Aunt Claire said, her eyes sparkling with irritation.

Like they'd been cast for the movie, they stood side-by-side and stared at her, speaking in unison. "What?"

Clark roared with laughter, reveling in the familiar banter and teasing. Mitch also chuckled.

Aunt Claire swung her attention to Clark's date. "And who are you, young man?"

"Oh, sorry," Clark said, recovering from his amusement. "Claire Ramsey, this is my date, Mitch Hampton."

Mitch stepped forward. "A pleasure to meet you, ma'am." In the same manner he had with Grace, he kissed her hand.

"So polite." She giggled. "I'm sure the pleasure is all mine."

Raising his gaze to his cousins, Clark clasped Duncan on the shoulder. "This is Duncan, and that's his brother Leif."

"Not the Tweedle brothers?" Mitch quirked a grin.

Leif chuckled. "Not most of the time." He shot Clark a strained grin. "We should get together sometime soon, Clark."

"Oh, sure, cuz," Clark replied, catching something amiss in the way Leif looked at him. "Let's grab a drink later."

"Great." Leif's grin turned genuine. "And it's nice to meet you, Mitch. Clark's told us so *nothing* about you."

The escort grinned. "Well, I heard you guys are both firefighters."

"Yes, they are," Aunt Claire confirmed, pride dripping from each word. "Duncan is a chief in Lake Forest Park, and Leif is at the White Center station."

"North versus South?" Mitch asked, addressing Duncan.

"Nah," Duncan chuckled, messing his younger brother's hair. "We already know which station's the best."

Leif narrowed his eyes. "Careful. All that hot air might start a fire, and I'm off duty."

While the brothers jostled each other good-naturedly, Clark surveyed the room. His gaze fell on Wes speaking to Grace. When Grace turned to Dan, Wes shot a worried glance toward Mitch. He noticed Clark watching and gave a half-hearted grin before turning back to the minister.

His aunt's voice brought his attention away from Wes. "Clark, sweetheart, we're going to find your parents. I hope we'll see you and Mitch later on."

"Absolutely, Aunt Claire." He gave her a kiss on the cheek and hugged his cousins. "See you later, guys."

"Catch ya later, right?" Leif asked, all serious behind his smile.

"I'm looking forward to that drink," Clark replied with a nod. He narrowed his eyes briefly at Leif, but his cousin just smiled. Once the Ramseys moved on and mingled with the other guests, Clark turned to Mitch. "Leif isn't usually so serious. He must have something big to tell me."

His thoughts returned to Wes, and his gaze sought him out in the room again. The man continued to stand with Dan and Grace talking to Reverend Randy. Wes shot furtive glances at Mitch every chance he got.

Clark scanned the room for a more secluded spot. Something was up between Mitch and Wes, and he needed to know what. A spot by the window was devoid of people, so Clark snagged his hired date's hand and led him through the clusters of guests.

Once they reached the relative quiet of the corner, Clark turned to Mitch. "What's going on with you and Wes?"

Mitch shrugged, but the smile returned. "I don't know. What gives you the impression something is?"

Scanning the room, Clark found and stared at the groom's brother again. "He stiffened when he first saw you, and just now he looked scared. Have you met him before?" No, scared wasn't quite the right word to describe the look the two men had shared.

Wes laughed at something the minister said, and then, once again, he glanced back at them. Eyes widening, his face went pale when he met Clark's gaze. With a forced smile, Wes said something to Grace and scurried from the room.

Tugging Clark's arm, Mitch lowered his voice and leaned toward Clark. "You might want to go see if he's okay."

Clark turned back to find no sign of Wes. "Did you see where he went?"

Wrapping an arm around his waist, Mitch squeezed him. "I'm guessing he's probably in the bathroom heaving his guts out from nerves."

Though enjoying the affection and warmth of Mitch's embrace, Clark frowned. "Why? He looked fine a moment ago."

With another sigh, Mitch gave him a small squeeze and released him. "He's likely assuming..." Mitch stopped. "Just go see if he's okay. You're the one who should do it. Trust me."

Meeting his date's gaze for a moment, Clark gave him a quick peck on his cheek and nodded. Still none the wiser about whatever history the two men might have, Clark figured Mitch wasn't going to tell him. "Will you be okay?"

Chuckling, Mitch grinned. "Yeah, I can take care of myself."

"Okay, I'll be right back." He wove his way toward the entrance of the large room. Stepping into the hallway, he found his way to the men's restroom, where he could hear loud retching through the door.

"Oh, boy." Clark's own stomach tightened. Did the poor guy have food poisoning? But Mitch had said Wes was *assuming…* Assuming what?

He inched open the door and stepped inside. The second stall door hung open, and Wes stared into the bowl of the toilet, his hands pressed firmly against the floor tiles. Clark stood behind him, collecting the discarded bowtie and the stylish blazer from the floor. "Wes?"

The disheveled man flushed the toilet, sat heavily on the tiled floor with legs outstretched, and stared at his black dress shoes.

"Are you okay?"

Not making eye contact, Wes furrowed his brow. "Mitch told you, didn't he?"

"Told me what?" So, there was something.

"You're going to make me say it?" A tremor shook Wes. He wiped a wad of toilet paper across his lips and tossed it into the bowl. "Why did you bring him?"

"He's my date." The direction this conversation was taking made Clark's stomach do a couple somersaults of its own.

The anger in Wes's glare made Clark take a step back.

"Come on, Clark. Don't play coy. You know damned well what he is."

The warmth drained from Clark's face. "What…?" His eyes widened in realization. "Holy shit, you've hired him, too?" Clark clamped his hands to his mouth. *Smooth move, dumbass.*

"Shit." Wes hung his head. "He really didn't tell you, did he?"

"No, he didn't." Dropping his hands to his sides, Clark couldn't help but stare at Wes. Even with his skin pale and his face drawn from emptying the contents of his stomach, the man was stunning. Classically handsome, dark hair, and those sparkling eyes. Wesley Palucinski set Clark's heart aflutter.

Wes lifted his chin and stared with the same pleading look he'd given Mitch. "Please, Clark. My family can't find out about me and Mitch."

"Well, I'm sure as hell not going to tell them." Clark pressed his back against the stall wall. "Can you imagine the scandal if I told everyone I had to hire a date for my sister's wedding? My parents would lose their shit."

Misery rolled off Wes in waves. "I can't believe you had to hire someone."

With a snort, Clark hung the jacket on the door of the stall and smoothed out the silk of the tie. "At the moment, no one's interested in me."

His face reddening, Wes stared at his shoes again. "That's not true," he said softly.

Clark's brow furrowed. "Nah, I'm pretty sure I'd know."

Wes hesitated then shook his head. "I haven't been able to get you off my mind since the moment Grace introduced us."

Staring at the shaking man miserably plunked on the floor of the men's room, Clark's mind struggled to catch up to Wes's admission. His heart thudded inside his chest. "Why didn't you say something at the coffee shop?"

"I'm not out and asking you for a date wasn't really an option after that disaster of a dinner my parents threw." Keeping his gaze firmly planted on his shiny, black shoes, Wes hugged his arms around his torso. "I almost said something at the coffee shop, but I was too scared."

Something Clark understood all too well. Relief washed over him, and he smiled at Wes. "Look at me."

Wes slowly lifted his gaze, watering blue eyes staring upward.

Kneeling, Clark lay his hand on Wes's shoulder. "I'm definitely interested. You have nothing to be afraid of with either me or Mitch. He didn't tell me, even when I pressed."

A tear rolled down his check. "My family would freak if they found out. Probably disown me."

"I understand. Really, you don't have anything to fear." Clark snagged another wad of toilet paper from the dispenser and handed it to Wes. "Even if Grace suspects you're gay, she'd never say anything unless you said she could."

"Thanks." He accepted the make-shift tissue and wiped his eyes. "I hope you're right."

"I know I am." Clark stood and offered a hand. "How

about we get you off the floor and cleaned up. Tonight's the stag party, isn't it?"

"Yeah." He let out a miserable breath and frowned. "I'm not looking forward to it."

Clark grimaced. "Me either." The last thing he wanted was to spend an evening with Dan and his frat brothers. Still, he'd enjoy seeing Dan squirm having two gay guys in the room. He quirked his eyebrow, a deliciously dirty thought coming to his mind. He waggled his eyebrows. "Perhaps we can have an after party with Mitch in our room."

"I don't know. I share a room with Dan." The frown deepened. "He'll be expecting me to come back after the party."

Clark shrugged. "Totally up to you. The offer's open for the whole weekend." He winked at Wes. "I don't mind sharing."

A glimmer of interest shone from Wes's eyes. "Do you think Mitch would be okay with that?"

Clark laughed. "I'd be surprised if he wasn't, but I'll make sure to clear it with him before we head to the bar. He did make the suggestion when we first met about hooking up with someone else at the wedding."

Gripping Clark's hand, Wes pulled himself from the floor. With a chuckle, the other man grabbed one more wad of toilet paper and wiped his face. "With a drink in me, I'll probably say yes."

"Either way, I'd really enjoy a date once we're back in Seattle." Standing next to Wes in front of the sink, Clark admired their reflections. "If you were serious about what you said…"

With a nod, Wes moved to the counter. "Yes, I am."

Clark stepped next to him and stared into the mirror over the sink. Though slightly taller than Clark, Wes seemed to fit next to him. "We look pretty good standing together, don't you think?"

"You look amazing." He frowned at the mirror. "I, on the other hand, am a mess."

Clark chuckled. "You're not that bad. I'll snag you something to drink and be right back."

Wes gave him a lopsided grin Clark found adorable. "You're really sweet."

While Wes turned on the faucet and splashed water on his still pale face, Clark left the restroom and returned to the reception hall. Crossing the room, Clark paused when Mrs. Palucinski caught his eye. She narrowed her gaze and scowled before turning her back on him.

Bitch.

Moving through the crowd, he approached the bar and asked the bartender for a glass of seltzer water. While he waited, he scanned the room. Grace and Dan were still engaged in conversation with Reverend Randy. Dan's parents were huddled in a corner, speaking as Mrs. Palucinski glanced around the room. Her gaze again fell on Clark, and the scowl returned.

How could that shrew be Wes's mother? He grinned and blew her a kiss.

She stiffened, eyes nearly bulging in fury, and then she swung away from him, again.

Clark turned his attention to the bartender who openly laughed. She pushed the seltzer water toward him. "She's a real piece of work, isn't she?"

"Yeah. I don't envy my sister having that as a mother-in-law." He pulled his wallet from his pocket and tossed a couple dollars in the pitcher serving as a tip jar.

The bartender grinned. "Thanks."

Pushing away from the bar, Clark wove back through the crowd toward the restrooms. He caught Mitch's eye just before he left the room. His date was in conversation with his parents. A flutter of anxiety swept over Clark, but Mitch smiled at him. Clark gave him a thumbs-up and left the room.

When Clark entered the men's room, he noted that color had returned to Wes's face. "This should help settle your stomach."

Accepting the glass, Wes took a sip. "Thanks."

Clark leaned against the sink. "Ready to face the roomful of family and friends excited for this shit-show?"

Chuckling, Wes took another sip of the seltzer. "No, but I really need to be."

Clark pushed himself up. "Come on. Let's go out there and surreptitiously flirt with each other."

Wes stepped into the hallway and paused before heading back to the reception. "I appreciate your kindness."

"Not a problem." Glancing around, he leaned in closer to Wes. "Remember, you have something on me now."

Wes nodded. "Your family would handle it better than mine would." He took another sip of the water.

Entering the crowd of guests, Clark scanned the room. "Where's Mitch?" His gaze settled on a group of older women surrounding his date and cackling as he chatted with them. "Oh, boy. He's with Mom and her gossip circle."

Wes rolled his eyes. "And there's my mother circling like a hawk about to snatch up a field mouse. You'd better go rescue him while I get back to Grace and Dan."

A smirk settled on Clark's lips. "Should be easy. She probably thinks I have the plague or something."

Smiling, Wes nodded. "Likely. See you later tonight."

Clark returned the grin. "Looking forward to it."

WES TOOK A breath and stepped into the Full Swing Bar in an alley off of Commercial Avenue. Loud music from the live band blared through an amp, and the place was packed. Spying his brother, he shifted into "straight mode", putting the earlier discussion with Clark and his own trysts with Mitch as far out of his mind as he could in order to concentrate on his not-gay persona.

"Hey, bro!" Dan rushed forward, a grin on his face and two beers in his hands. "Have a cold one." His brother thrust the pint at him. "I'm getting married in the morning. Drink up." He clinked his glass with Wes's and draped an arm across his shoulders.

Taking a swallow of the amber, he caught a glimpse of Mitch chatting with a couple of Dan's frat brothers. A surge of nerves shook him as he considered what the evening had to offer with Grace's handsome brother and the escort. He took a deeper swig from the glass.

His brother grinned at him. "I still can't believe Gracie

said yes."

"I can't either," Wes agreed, annoyance dripping off each word.

Eyeing him, Dan gave him a squeeze and released him. "It's your turn, bro."

Inwardly cringing, Wes readied himself for the onslaught from his brother. "I'm good."

"You don't want to be single the rest of your life, do you?" Dan frowned. "There's lots of hot fish in the sea. Half of Grace's sorority sisters were looking you over at the reception. What about that Chelsea?"

Wes's mind drifted to the gaggle of sorority women he'd been surrounded by that afternoon. Chelsea was a blonde bombshell. Smart, witty—and she'd shoved her boobs against his chest while pretending to trip. "Nah, really. I'm good."

"I'll help you, bro. I got your back." He turned toward the bar and nodded at a woman decked out in a leather skirt with a pink blouse, fishnets, and stiletto heels. "Amy, there, is the bomb. She'll rock your world."

Wes narrowed his gaze at this brother. "And how would you know that?"

Dan laughed. "Not firsthand. She's legendary with my frat. I'll go get her."

"No." Wes surprised himself with how forceful the word came out.

With his frown deepening, Dan turned back to him. "What's up with you, Wes? You turn down every offer I make to hook you up."

"I appreciate the effort, but you and I have very different tastes in…*partners*." He chugged the last of the beer.

Before Dan could say anything further, the men's room door opened to Wes's right, and Clark stepped into the bar. Wes grinned, eager to ditch the straight guys and head back to Mitch and Clark's room. "Glad you're here, Clark," Wes said as the man drew nearer.

"Glad to be included." Clark shot a quick glance at Dan then returned his attention to Wes. "I haven't spent much time up here in Anacortes." Clark glanced around the bar and waved over to Mitch. Wes followed his gaze and nodded at the escort.

Sticking out his hand, Dan caught Clark's attention. "Guess after tomorrow we're all going to be brothers." The comment was so forced Wes had to stifle a laugh.

Clark grasped the offered hand and shook it. "Nice of you to see it that way. I hope you and Grace have a long and happy marriage." Clark smiled at his nearly-brother-in-law, and Wes noted he seemed to be sincere in his sentiment.

Mitch sauntered over with a glass of red wine. "Hey there, I was beginning to wonder if you'd ditched me for one of Dan's frat brothers." He gave Clark a quick peck on the cheek. "I got this for you."

Taking the offered glass, Clark smiled at his date. "Thanks."

A pang of guilt accompanied another inward cringe. Not at Mitch and his gentlemanly actions. At least, not so much for that. Wes knew he was paid for being charming. More the idea that Clark felt fully comfortable being himself, and nobody except Wes's family even batted an eyelash. *Fuck it. After this weekend, I'm telling my brother I'm gay.*

Frowning, Dan threw back the rest of his pint. With a loud belch, he nodded at the three of them. "Have a good time, guys. Guess there's going to be some fine entertainment later." He wriggled his eyebrows at his brother. "And her name's Amy."

Dan swaggered off to join his friends while Wes rolled his eyes and faced Clark and Mitch. "I need a stronger drink."

The three men approached the bar. Clark's cousin Leif, dressed in a red button-up, short-sleeved shirt and a pair of deep blue jeans, grinned at them. Wes tried not to focus on the firefighter's bulging muscles barely held in by the lightweight shirt. *No use getting hot and bothered by a straight guy. Besides...* He glanced at Clark and Mitch, both dressed to kill. *I'll get the guys I want tonight after this fucking bachelor party.*

"Hey, Clark." Leif hugged his cousin.

"Hey, cuz. You remember Mitch, right?" Clark asked, stepping out of the hug and turning toward his date.

"Sure do." Leif extended his hand, the hint of pink painting his face. "Nice to see you again."

"Likewise," Mitch replied with a grin. "I'm sure a good lookin' guy like you is lighting fires all over this wedding."

Color blossomed deeper on Leif's cheeks. He gave a shake of his head. "I put out fires. I don't ignite them."

Clark winked at his date. "I'll douse your *three*-alarm fire later."

The three of them laughed, and Wes allowed a chuckle. He stood quietly, watching the comfortable exchange, wishing like hell he could have this. An accepting family, a boyfriend, and the easy banter that came with being out and comfortable. Not that Mitch was Clark's boyfriend, but Leif didn't know that.

Clasping a hand on Wes's shoulder, Clark addressed Leif. "This is Wes, the groom's brother." The hand on his shoulder squeezed. "We like him."

Leif stuck out his hand. "Good to see you again. Grace introduced us at the reception this afternoon." He glanced at Clark while shaking Wes's hand. "You don't like Dan?" He let go and gave his cousin a sharp stare.

Wes found himself staring at Clark as well. Knowing the backstory to Clark's comment, Wes couldn't blame the guy for despising his brother and his parents.

Lifting his hand from Wes's shoulder, Clark shrugged. "He and I don't get along. At all. I gather I'm not all that popular with Wes's parents either."

Understatement. The conversation Wes had with his mother that morning still stung. She'd railed over *the gay* and his evil ways, warning Wes to stay clear of him. He smirked in satisfaction. Not only was he keeping company with Clark and his date, but, later, he'd get the chance to spend the night with both of them. He could hardly wait to ditch the bar and head out.

Mitch laughed. "I saw you blow Mrs. Palucinski a kiss at the reception. She looked ready to explode before she turned away."

With a groan, Wes shook his head. "I'll hear about that later."

Clark winked. "I'll make it up to you."

Fighting another blush, Wes stepped to the bar and flagged the bartender. "Whiskey, please." He sat on one of the stools, surveying the bar while Clark and Mitch continued their conversation with Leif. Dan caught his gaze and grinned, nodding at Amy. Wes cringed and gave a slight shake of his head. Why couldn't his brother leave him alone? Amy was the last person he wanted.

Locking his gaze on Wes, Dan lifted a shot glass in toast and downed the contents.

When his whiskey arrived, Wes caught his brother's gaze again and silently toasted. The whiskey went down warm, but the alcohol made him grimace and give a little shake.

Dan laughed and turned to the bartender, tilting his head toward Wes. The bartender nodded and a moment later, another shot of whiskey slid in front of Wes.

The music changed, and Amy twirled around the bar, shimmying against various guys until she reached Wes. She smirked then pressed her breasts against his chest and her arms to his shoulders.

"Sorry," she muttered close to Wes's ear. "Your brother insisted. No worries though. I can tell you don't swing that way." When she leaned back, she winked.

He stiffened. "Shit," he breathed. When had he become so transparent? Holy fuck, did Dan suspect he wasn't straight? Maybe this was a test.

"Just go along with it, sugar," she cooed. "Give him a good show, and he'll never guess. I'll help you." She ground against him. "Now, smile and put your hands on my ass."

Wes jerked, beginning to feel nauseous. "What?"

Amy grabbed his hands and planted them firmly on her soft butt. Then she leaned back and gave a teasing yelp. "Oh!"

The bar erupted in cheers and catcalls. One of Dan's frat brothers shouted out, half sloshed, "Yeah, Wesley! Give her a kiss!"

Dan stared expectantly, nodding with a shit-eating grin. "Now's your chance, bro!" he yelled.

Amy moved backward and pulled him off the barstool. Then she pressed close again and wrapped her wrists around the back of his neck, pulling him in. "Just a quick one, and that'll be it, promise."

"Thanks," he breathed, grateful she got him and his need to stay "straight". He gave her a closed-mouth peck on the lips. The room exploded again in cheers.

She laughed, slowly pulling away and wagging a finger at him like he'd been naughty. She grinned with an exaggerated wink, and then spun and stalked another guy on the other side of the room.

Wes slapped the bar, fighting the bile in his throat and pointing at the empty shot glass. The bartender nodded, his gaze sympathetic. Wes glanced at Clark, Mitch, and Leif. The trio stood staring at him, mouths slightly open.

"Fuck," Wes muttered, slumping his shoulders. Embarrassment burned hot from his head to his toes. He turned back to the bar and found the whiskey shot. Without hesitation, he grasped the glass and pounded back the drink.

WHILE MITCH PARKED the car in the hotel's outdoor parking lot, Clark supported a stumbling Wes, guiding him through the lobby. With an arm hanging over Clark's shoulder, the two men staggered to the elevator. Once inside, Wes slung his other arm around Clark's waist and hugged him. "Thank you."

Clark shuddered, both excited and guarded at the warmth of Wes's embrace. "No problem. Do you want to go back to your room?"

With a shake of his head, Wes planted a kiss on Clark's neck. "I'm a little drunk, and this might be the only time we do this, but I want to take you up on your offer. I want both of you."

"Are you sure?" As much as he wanted Wes, he didn't want to get him in trouble with Dan. With Wes drunk, he was also worried about potential morning-after regrets.

"Yeah," he slurred. "Dan'll think I went off with Amy."

The elevator opened when it reached the fifth floor, and they stumbled into the hallway. Fortunately, the wedding party, which Clark was not a part of, had the third floor of the hotel, so the coast was clear. Clark slipped his keycard into the lock and opened the door to his room. Helping his companion into a chair, he poured a glass of water. "Drink this."

Wes took the glass and gulped it down. As he finished, the door swung open, and Mitch stood there with a smile on his face.

"I thought you two would've started by now."

Wes set the glass on the table beside him. "We're waiting for you, stud."

Snatching up the *Do Not Disturb* sign and placing it on the outside handle, Mitch bumped the door closed with his hip and turned the lock. Then he abandoned his silk shirt and unbuttoned his jeans, teasing the zipper downward.

Clark's temperature rose. As his date revealed more of his pale skin by inching the denim down his muscular legs, Clark glanced at their other companion.

Wes was fully engaged with events, the water helping to sober his drunken state.

Returning his attention to the striptease in front of him, Clark let out a low whistle when Mitch shucked his briefs and stood naked before them. He stroked his large cock that jutted from a neat patch of trimmed, red hair.

Wes's hand went to the crotch of his jeans. "Fuck, I never get tired of the sight of that monster."

Mitch chuckled. "You love it ramming your ass, too."

With a loud moan, Wes used his palm to press down on his cock. "And you'd better give it to me good tonight."

Clark's eyes widened, and his breath hitched. *He's a bottom?* He recovered his composure and stood in front of Wes. After sliding his hands down his body, Clark quickly stripped off his own clothes. "See anything you like?" he asked, feeling a little breathless.

Wes nodded and reached out to stroke Clark's stiff shaft. Still seated, he pulled Clark closer and wrapped his lips around the head.

Liquid fire surged through Clark at the exquisite

warmth surrounding his cock and the greedy tongue probing his slit. Mitch moved to stand behind Clark, kissing and nibbling his neck, while grinding his erection against his ass. Clark shook from the multiple sources of pleasure causing ripples to shiver through his body.

Wes let Clark's shaft slide from his mouth and stood, weaving slightly. He guided both men onto the bed. Standing before them, Wes swayed and caught himself before he fell. He loosened his tie, unbuttoned and pushed his shirt away from his torso, and unclasped his pants. The denim hugged his hips as he fished his cock from the boxers and let it hang out.

Clark's cock pulsed at the sight of the man's beautiful body. A light dusting of curly, dark hair stretched between his quarter-sized nipples. A treasure trail led from his bellybutton to a thick thatch of lighter brown hair surrounding his cock and large balls.

Clark pushed down Wes's jeans and underwear to the floor, pausing a moment to give the thick, veiny cock a kiss on the head. Using the unknotted tie, he pulled the naked man onto the bed. Wes lay on top of Clark, and they kissed.

Hearing the tear of a condom package and the squirt of lube, Clark wrapped his arms around Wes and pulled him deeper into the kiss. Soft and sensuous gave way to hunger and passion, their tongues dueling for entry into each other's mouths. Wes pushed his tongue deeper, exploring with soft whimpers.

Gasping, Clark broke the kiss, struggling to get his breath. Wes nuzzled against his neck and alternated between soft bites and licking the tender skin, paralyzing Clark with waves of pleasure.

The bed shifted, and Wes gasped. "Yeah, Mitch. Give it to me."

Clark looked around Wes to find Mitch slowly driving home his erection into the Wes's ass. "You've got it all."

With his eyes closed, a lusty moan escaped Wes's lips. "Fuck, I love your cock in me."

Wriggling out from under Wes as Mitch established a steady rhythm, Clark pulled himself to his knees and offered his hardness to Wes. Wes eagerly sucked in the head and shaft, gagging when he tried to take too much.

Clark chuckled, stroking Wes's hair. "Easy, baby. It's not going anywhere."

Backing off slightly, Wes worked the slit with his tongue. The delicious warmth wrapping around his shaft made Clark's balls begin to tingle. He let Wes work over his cock for a few moments until the tingling turned into an imminent signal of his orgasm.

Clark sat back, pulling his dick from Wes's mouth and sucking in air trying to stave off his release. "Oh, shit that felt good."

Still taking Mitch's fucking, Wes reached for Clark. "Why did you stop?"

"You were going to make me shoot." He leaned forward, catching Wes's face in his hands and kissing him. Their tongues dueled again, and Wes moaned into Clark's mouth as Mitch increased his pounding.

With a gasp, Mitch paused in his fucking. "Damn, you boys look hot making out like that. Now, I need a break." He gently eased out of Wes and sat back.

Clark broke the kiss and nearly lost himself in Wes's gaze. "Can I be inside you?"

With a nod, Wes closed in for a quick kiss. "Please. I want you."

Leaning back and pushing himself off the bed, Clark grabbed a condom from the nightstand. He ripped the package and rolled the rubber onto his fully erect cock.

"I want you, Clark," Wes repeated in a murmur, wriggling his butt invitingly.

Mitch moved aside, and Clark stepped to the bed, lined up his head to Wes's ass, and slid slowly inside. Even after Mitch's thick monster, Wes's pucker remained tight.

Wes threw back his head. "You feel amazing."

The tingling started again. "I'm not going to last long." Clark hissed between his teeth, heat squeezing around him.

"That's okay," Wes groaned. "Take me."

When Wes tightened his muscles, a jolt of pleasure shot through Clark, intensifying the sensation of his impending orgasm.

Grabbing hold of Wes's shoulder, Clark pounded him harder until he couldn't wait any longer. "I'm gonna shoot."

"Give it to me, Clark." Wes ground his ass against Clark's groin, pulling Clark's cock in deeper.

Screwing his eyes shut, Clark felt the familiar rush and roared out his passion. Shot after shot filled the condom inside Wes. After several gasping breaths, Clark pulled out of Wes's still quivering ass and fell back onto his heels, concentrating on his breathing and trying to keep from falling over.

Mitch took his place. "I want to make you come."

Nodding, Wes flipped onto his back and brought his knees to his chest. "Do it."

With a lustful grin, Mitch drilled in deep.

"Oh, fuck yeah!" Wes cried out. His back arched, and he stroked his cock twice. With a yell, Wes unloaded, his come splashing against his chest and stomach.

Flinging back his head, Mitch rammed deep and roared out his release, muscles straining. After falling forward onto shaky arms and kissing Wes deeply, Mitch pulled out and rolled onto the bed.

A steady stream of "thank you" and "so amazing" poured from Wes, trailing off when his eyes drifted closed and he relaxed into the sheets.

Clark took both of their used condoms, tied them off, and dropped them to the floor. He grabbed his briefs and wiped off the mess from Wes's torso.

"Mmm, thanks," Wes murmured, nearly asleep.

Clark tossed away the underwear and cuddled with Mitch, wrapping an arm around him. "Thanks for this."

Mitch shifted, pressing his back against Clark. "Thank you. Now, let's get some sleep," the deep, sexy voice rumbled sleepily. "Big day tomorrow."

CHAPTER SEVEN

THE BRIGHT LIGHT coming in the room from the open curtain stung Wes's eyes, and he slung his arm over his face in an unsuccessful attempt to restore the cool darkness. A pounding behind his eyes made him regret all those whiskey shots, both with, and because of, his brother at the bar last night.

"Good morning." Mitch's deep voice rumbled next to him.

Wes groaned. "Can someone turn down the sun? Too bright."

The bed moved for a moment, and blissfully cool darkness took the place of the unrelenting morning sun.

Warmth returned as Mitch crawled back into bed. "You look like you're having some trouble rising." A large hand caressed his thigh, ghosting along the fuzz on the inside of his leg and brushing against his balls.

Pressure surged through his hardening cock, and Clark's voice drifted over the escort. "No, he's not." The bed shifted again, and the warm wetness of one of their mouths engulfed his shaft.

Chuckling, Wes moved back his arm to see Clark's wavy hair bouncing while he gently sucked. "I've got a throbbing headache, but this helps."

Mitch continued to caress his leg. "We'll get you some water in a bit. I think Clark's intent on getting a drink first."

Pausing, Clark winked at Wes. "You had enough to drink for all of us last night." He resumed his sucking while Mitch brushed his lips along Wes's neck. "And some hot, straight action."

"Oh, God, don't remind me." He closed his eyes again, savoring the contact and the pleasure from these two men, and trying not to think about Amy. Reaching down, his fingers slid into Clark's silken hair, while Mitch kissed his way down Wes's chest and flicked his tongue onto his erect nipple.

A jolt of sensitivity made him gasp and arch his back. "Fu-u-uck…" Wes moaned.

Mitch continued nibbling and sucking, and Clark's expert blowjob coaxed his orgasm closer. The tingling in his balls intensified, and his body went rigid. Clark pulled off and stroked Wes the rest of the way, geysers flying and splashing onto Wes's chest. Clark returned to a light suckling as a spent Wes rested on the sheets.

Between the tremors of his post orgasm and the over-stimulation of his nipples and head, Wes could barely move. His headache subsided significantly.

With a groan, he pushed Mitch off his chest and tensed when Clark took another swipe across his glands. "Oh, man, you gotta stop."

Grinning, Clark gave one final lap and rolled to his side. His erection rested against abdomen, slowly deflating but still twitching from his release.

Mitch rose from the pile of sweaty bodies and stood with his chubbed cock facing them. "After I get you that glass of water, we can start round two."

Three loud raps at the door made them all jump.

"Shit," Wes swore. Terror cancelled out any afterglow from their coupling. He scrambled off the bed and into the bathroom. The cold bathroom tiles beneath his feet chilled him as much as the possibility of being discovered. He peeked out, watching Mitch slip on a robe from the closet and open the door.

Dan's hesitant voice floated into the room. "Hi, uh…"

"Mitch," the escort said evenly.

"Mitch. Sorry to bother you. I was wondering if you'd seen my brother. He didn't come back to the room last night, and I can't find him anywhere in the hotel." He heard Dan shuffle at the door. "I thought he hooked up with Amy, but—"

Wes held his breath at the pause.

The sound of sharp inward breath filled the silence. "*Is that his shirt?*"

DRAWING COVERS OVER his nakedness, Clark stared at the door framing the groom. His erection quickly sagged, and his gaze shifted to the three sets of discarded party clothes strewn about the room, guiltily intermingled in a line from the door to the two used condoms next to the bed.

His future brother-in-law's eyes followed the same line, his brow furrowing deeper the farther into the room his gaze went. He stared at Mitch, his question hanging in the air.

Shrugging, Mitch glanced at the floor. "The poor guy was so drunk last night that he crashed here on the couch. You weren't back, and we were afraid to leave him alone."

Wes emerged from the bathroom with a towel wrapped around his waist. The hand not clutching the towel shook, but he resolutely stepped into his brother's line of sight. "You don't need to cover for me, Mitch."

"Wes, what are you doing in here with these guys?" Dan's eyes narrowed, zeroing in on Wes's bellybutton where a few white globs clung to short hairs. "Did they take advantage of you?"

Stepping in front of Dan, Mitch blocked his view into the room, arms bulging out of the rolled-up sleeves of the robe. "And exactly what do you mean by that?" The low menace in his voice made Clark flinch.

It had a similar effect on Dan. "Uh, well, he was drunk, right?" Dan spluttered. "I know what you gay guys fantasize about doing to drunk straight—"

Mitch's body trembled, and he grabbed a fistful of Dan's shirt, hefting him onto his tiptoes. His jaw tightened. "This gay guy is going to give your homophobic face a memento for your wedding pictures if you don't shut the fuck up, right now." The muscles bulged in his arm, lifting Dan higher off the ground. He cocked his other arm back, ready to deliver a formidable fist.

Dan's face was a mask of terror, peering wide-eyed at Clark over Mitch's head.

Oh my God. Clark imagined how he was going to

explain this scene to his sister. Last night, he could easily have said no to Wes staying over, erring on the side of caution. Now, he had to deal with an angry escort, a terrified groom, and a sister who would likely prove to be the opposite of her name.

Wes intervened, hurrying to the door and using his free hand to gently push Mitch back. "Okay, that's enough." He turned to his brother. "Dan, we'll discuss this later. Suffice it to say, both of these guys were perfect gentlemen and didn't *force* me to do anything."

Mitch released Dan's shirt, and the groom stumbled back when his feet reconnected with the floor. "But your clothes are all over the place, and the rubbers by the bed…" he wailed, a tinge of hysteria in his voice.

"That's right, Dan," Wes said slowly, struggling to keep his patience. "Go back to our room. I'll be there shortly." Wes shoved Dan into the hallway, letting the door slam in his brother's gaping face.

Nostrils flaring, Mitch strode to the bed and plunked onto the edge. "That fucking piece of shit!" His fair skin reddened from his shoulders to the top of his head.

Clark rose and rubbed his hand over Mitch's trembling back. "Take a few deep breaths and calm down."

Wes joined them, sitting next to Mitch. "I'm really sorry, guys. I basically just came out to him, and I don't think he's taking it well." He glanced at the clothes on the floor. "I guess I'd better get dressed and face the music."

Still rubbing Mitch's back, Clark turned to Wes. "Do you want one of us to come with you?"

After using the towel to wipe off the remnants of

Clark's blowjob, Wes stood and let the towel drop. He bent over and dug into the pile of clothes, tossing aside Clark's underwear before retrieving his own. "No, I'd better handle this alone." He stepped into his briefs and pulled them up. "The worst he can do is tell my parents, but hopefully he's in enough shock to do what I told him and wait for me."

With a frown, Clark stood, leaving Mitch on the bed, and crossed to Wes. "Do you really think he'd out you to your folks?"

Wes slipped on his shirt, and his fingers worked swiftly over the buttons. "I honestly don't know." He bent over to grab his jeans.

"If things get bad, you can come back here," Clark offered. "I don't mind if you stay with us." His gaze turned to the other man in the room. "Mitch?"

"Of course, I don't mind," Mitch growled, his chest still heaving. "Don't stay with that homophobe. You don't need to put up with his crap." The still fuming escort nearly spat out his words.

After tugging on his pants, Wes stood tall. "I won't." He leaned in and kissed Clark, and then strode to the bed and gave Mitch a peck on the cheek. "Time to be who I really am."

SUMMONING HIS COURAGE, Wes slipped the keycard though the slot and opened the door to the room he shared with his brother. "Dan?"

"Yeah," Dan's subdued voice replied. He stood at the

window, looking out over the streets of Anacortes with his arms crossed. The early morning sunshine cast a warm glow into the room in stark contrast to the chilly reception.

With some hesitancy, Wes continued into the room, letting the door close behind him. "You want to talk?"

Dan clenched his jaw and continued staring out the window. "Did those guys rape you?"

Rolling his eyes, Wes crossed the room and sat on the edge of one of the queen beds. "No, they didn't. Everything we did together, I wanted."

Turning away from the window, Dan's mouth parted for a moment, shock and confusion evident on his face. "You're not gay. I know you're not gay."

"Do you?" Wes shook his head. "You actually don't know all that much about my life since I moved away from home. You haven't asked."

His frown deepened. "But why didn't you tell me?"

Wes puffed out a sharp breath. "Did you hear what you said to Mitch? Do you understand why you almost got socked in the face?" He glared at his brother. "You couldn't even shake Clark's hand yesterday without flinching like you'd touched something diseased and repulsive." His voice rose in both pitch and volume, anger boiling while all the years of Dan's rude and ignorant behavior bubbled to the fore. "You can't say one nice thing about gay people. Why the hell would I come out to you, knowing how you feel?"

Dan's face paled. He uncrossed his arms and took a step back, reaching for one of the chairs. For all his bluster, his brother had always been the weaker of the two of them. If he'd received criticism, Wes had always been there to soothe his battered pride or bolster his confidence.

"But last night, we were talking about you getting married and settling down," Dan spluttered.

"*You* were talking about that," Wes said. "I was just along for the ride."

"But that lap dance—"

Wes cut him off. "Yeah, asshole. You set her on me, but she already had me figured out." His mind flashed back to the closed-mouth kiss, and he cringed. At least she hadn't insisted on a make-out session before moving on.

"You kissed her," Dan shot back.

"To keep *you* from hounding me all night." Wes's hands shook with anger, but he balled his fist, trying to keep his fury in check.

"But, bro, this isn't you." Shaking his head, Dan turned away from Wes. "Those damned fags are trying to turn you, just like Mom said they would. Clark and Mitch were right behind you all evening."

With his face burning, Wes glared at his brother. "I should've let Mitch deck you. I'm not willing to deal with your hateful bullshit anymore." He rose, strode to the closet, and began pulling out his overnight bag.

Dan's face fell. "What are you doing?"

"Don't worry. Your *faggot* brother won't ruin your wedding," Wes seethed. "I'll keep the 'straight best man' act going for you until today is over, but after the reception, we're done. I warned you, but you couldn't let your prejudice go. Maybe, someday, if you can get over

Mom and Dad's brainwashing, we can be brothers again."

"Wes, wait," Dan said, his tone pleading.

Wes snagged the last of his clothes out of the closet and stuffed them into the bag. Swinging around to face Dan, he hefted the strap over his shoulder and grabbed the garment bag holding his tux. "Just so you know, I've been fucking around with guys since I was fourteen." Glaring at his brother's shell-shocked and gaping face, he reached for the doorknob. "If you want to tell Mom and Dad, go ahead. I don't fucking care anymore. I'd wait until after the reception, but it's up to you."

"Aw, come on, bro," Dan said, his mouth set into a miserable frown. He took a tentative step toward Wes.

Yanking open the door, Wes glared. "Fuck you." Striding into the hallway, he let the door slam behind him.

AFTER TEXTING GRACE and asking her to come to his room, Clark fidgeted, his dread weighing heavy on his shoulders. Three raps at the door, just like her fiancé's earlier that morning, made Clark jump with a start. He pushed off the bed and rushed to greet his sister.

She stood in the hallway wrapped in a terrycloth robe and sporting full makeup. Her long, blonde hair was partially braided in the back and wrapped around the top of her head. A silver clip he recognized as their great-grandmother's held the bun in place. She looked stunning, and he had second thoughts about telling her what had happened with Dan.

She grinned from ear to ear. "Good morning, and

welcome to my wedding day!" She beamed happiness.

Oh boy. Steeling himself, he held the door open for his sister. "Come in. We need to talk."

Bustling into the room, she cocked an immaculately sculpted eyebrow. "What about? And where's that hunky Mitch?"

"I sent him out to take a walk and cool down. Before I start, I need to swear you to secrecy." His stomach sank, and he watched her face lose its happy expression.

She stared at him, her brow furrowing. "Did you two have a fight?"

"Not with each other," Clark hedged.

She surveyed his face and settled her hands onto her hips. "You're about to drop some bombshell on me, aren't you?"

With a sigh, he nodded. She could always read him, especially when they were kids. She'd pried out every secret he'd ever had, but she'd always kept her mouth shut.

Pursing her lips, she crossed her arms. "Do you *have* to do this on my wedding day?"

Pangs of guilt hit him, but he had to tell her what had happened before anyone else did, or worse, before she heard it from the Palucinskis. "Unfortunately."

Continuing across the room, she settled onto one of the overstuffed chairs and crossed her legs. "Okay, I swear not to say anything. What's going on?"

"Well, first thing, Wes is gay," he said and held his breath.

She laughed. "Oh, honey, I already know that. It's so obvious." Her eyes widened, and she leaned forward. "Did you cheat on Mitch by getting into Wes's pants?"

He winced. "No cheating involved. He spent the night with us last night." He quickly added, "And it was completely consensual."

"I would never have doubted that." Raising her hands above her head like she was in a revival meeting, she grinned. "Finally, the boy knows who he is."

"For him, I don't think that was ever in doubt." He took a breath. "Here's the part where you're not going to be so happy."

Her smile evaporated, and her face settled into a neutral stare. "Dan found out."

"Yup." His stomach tightened, knowing he hadn't told her the worst of it yet and dreading her reaction.

She brought her hand to her forehead but pulled it away before she touched her makeup. "Oh, God, what did he say?"

Taking a deep breath and puffing it out, Clark fought the ache in his stomach and his fraying nerves. "He basically accused us of date-raping your future brother-in-law. Mitch was so angry he lifted your fiancé off the floor, but Wes got in between them before Dan got a black eye."

Launching from the chair, her face pinked in rising fury. "I've had conversations with him before about treating you with respect. He was warned about this weekend."

Clark held up his hands. "I know, Grace. Before you rip him apart, he'd just discovered his brother naked with two men instead of one of your sorority sisters. I'm sure that was a shock for him."

The pink deepened into red, and she clenched her fists. "Why would that be an excuse? Especially after that dinner."

Clark sighed. "It's not. It's an explanation."

"*Not. Good. Enough.*" With a shake of her head, she strode to the door. "One of the conditions of me going through with this marriage was him getting past his homophobia. I told that bastard over and over I wouldn't put up with it." She faced him with one hand on the doorknob. "Thanks. You've helped me realize what a mistake I'm making."

The heat drained from Clark's face. "Grace, you aren't calling off the wedding, are you?"

Her mouth tightened into a thin line. "Damned right, I am. Mom already warned me about him, and Daddy cautioned me to consider the differences in how we look at the world. But I thought I could change him." With a snort, she turned the knob and flung open the door.

"Now, Grace. Hold on—" Clark took a step toward her.

With an angry shake of her head, she said, "He's not going to get away with treating you like this, let alone his own brother."

Outside the door stood a startled Wes with his bag over his shoulder and a couple of fingers holding onto the hanger of his tuxedo. "Grace?" he asked, his eyes widening.

She flung her arms around him. "I'm sorry I'm not going to be your sister."

He gaped at Clark, nearly losing hold of his clothes. "What?"

Clark hurried to the doorway, but Grace had already released Wes and was storming down the hall. "I'm finished with your brother," she shouted, stalking away quickly.

Looking from Grace's retreating form to Clark, Wes cocked his head to one side. "What the hell just happened here?"

CHAPTER EIGHT

T HE BRIGHT MID-MORNING sun lit the brick buildings of the historic section of Anacortes, warming and giving the brick a red glow. Wes surveyed the shops along Commercial Avenue, many just opening. Though a lovely town decked out with murals on the walls facing side-streets and colorful canopies reaching over the sidewalk, he had a hard time enjoying the morning walk with Mitch and Clark. His brother's wedding was in tatters, due in no small part to Wes's inadvertent outing.

Stopping in front of the doorway to a bakery, Clark nodded his head. "This looks as good a place as any to talk."

Wes surveyed the shop as they stepped inside. Quaint wallpaper, a counter with pies and pastries, and a couple waitresses flitting between tables. Mitch guided them to a table by the window and, after a waitress brought over a pot of coffee, the three men huddled.

Hands wrapped around his steaming mug, Mitch shook his head. "I'm sorry I lost my cool, guys. Accusations like that make my blood boil. In my profession, I have to be really careful about sex and consent."

Wes patted his shoulder. "Don't worry about it. I

appreciate you defending both of our virtues."

Chuckling darkly, Clark sipped from his mug. "Definitely not your fault, Mitch."

The escort stared into his coffee. "Still. You didn't, um… *invite* me to scare the shit out of the groom."

Taking Mitch's hand, Wes gave it a squeeze. "Seriously. Don't worry about it." Letting go, he sat back and sighed. "So, I guess we're heading back to Seattle this morning. I have no desire to stay for the aftermath with my parents." He gave Clark a sad smile. "Can I hide out at your place for a few days?"

Clark met Wes's gaze, his expressive eyebrows lowering and arching, reflecting conflict between determination and sympathy. "Look, Wes. I don't think we should just cut and run. The real question is, can we fix this situation? I don't like how Dan spoke to us, but I don't dislike the guy, per se. He's probably a good match for Grace—if he can get over being such a douche."

"How can you say that?" Wes frowned, not quite believing Clark wanted to stay and help Dan. "She isn't going to deal with his anti-gay ranting. And with good reason." His face heated up thinking about all the hateful bullshit Dan constantly spewed about gays.

Clark nodded. "You're right, she won't. Maybe she can straighten him out."

With a shake of his head, Mitch snorted. "He's plenty straight right now."

Nodding, Wes sipped his coffee, still glowering over his brother's hateful rhetoric. "Grace can't fix him. My parents and their church did too good of a job. It's a waste of time trying. He doesn't want anything to do with people like us."

"Did he actually say that?" Clark lifted an eyebrow.

"Well, no," Wes conceded. "I told him to fuck off, though." He turned away and stared out the window. "Grace isn't the only one who's done with him." Replaying the scene in his mind, Wes's anger abated somewhat. He recalled his brother's eyes clouded with confusion. Dan had been more shocked than anything, and his brother hadn't outright rejected him. Replaying the discussion in his mind, Wes realized Dan had asked him not to go.

Clark addressed his date. "What about you, Mitch? Do you think we should help Dan and Grace get back together?"

With a shrug, Mitch stirred cream into his coffee. "I don't know, Clark. Seems to me she's making the right decision. But you two know them a lot better than I do. Yesterday, they seemed pretty happy together."

"I know she cares about him," Clark said. "He wouldn't have gotten this far with her if she didn't."

With a reluctant huff, Wes dragged his gaze from the window to stare at the two men. "If you really think this is the right thing to do, I suppose we should probably make sure the split is irreversible before they tell our parents."

Clark wrinkled his nose. "Not a ringing endorsement, but I'll take it." He lifted his cup. "You're right. Once Dad finds out, he's likely to take his own swing at Dan. Even at fifty-seven, he can pack a punch." He took another sip of coffee.

Wes's mind kept drifting back to the moment he'd

stormed out after Dan had asked him to wait. Grace would likely rip his parents to shreds over how Dan had treated Clark. Hopefully, she'd omit the part about Dan finding him naked with her brother and his date, because then Dan would have to explain what had happened.

Leaning back in his chair, Mitch clasped his hands behind his head. "I'll help out however I can, but I think you two should be the ones to get the unhappy couple to change their minds. Neither of them has any reason to listen to me. They don't know me."

Grudgingly, Wes nodded. "Okay, I'll give my jerk brother another chance." He stared at Clark, grim acceptance making his stomach knot. "I'm not talking to him first, though."

With a laugh, Mitch patted his leg. "Don't sound so excited. It shouldn't be me, either. I almost decked him last time."

"Yeah, I suppose I can handle Dan if you want to tackle Grace." Clark frowned. "You'll have your work cut out for you to change her mind."

Wes drained the remainder of his coffee and set the cup on the table. "Maybe I can at least get her to calm down."

Mitch leered at him. "If you boys manage to get the wedding back on, I'll make this evening extra special. You're staying with us tonight, right, Wes?"

A stirring in his crotch momentarily took his mind off their situation. He'd do about anything to get another night with the two of them. "I hope so."

"You are," Clark said with a definitive nod. "With that

incentive, I'll be going." He stood. "See you both later. I'll text when I'm bringing Dan back to our room."

Nodding, Wes watched Clark walk toward the door. The man exuded confidence, and he loved the way his sexy round ass moved in his jeans.

"Gonna be okay, Wesley?" Mitch asked with an arched brow.

"Yeah," Wes replied, grabbing the escort's hand and squeezed it.

Mitch returned his gesture with a wistful smile.

Though Wes loathed the idea of speaking to Dan again, he'd have to face his brother eventually. He did owe the man for making his meeting Clark possible. At least he had time to work through his anger by talking to Grace first.

NERVES FRAYED AND uncertain what to say, Clark knocked on Dan's door.

Footsteps approached. "Go away."

"Dan, it's Clark," he called through the closed door. "Can I come in?"

The door opened just enough for Dan to poke out his head. An angry red patch lit up his cheek, and three small scratches marred the side of his face. His wary gaze darted past Clark into the hallway. "Where's your boyfriend?"

"Out for a stroll." He glanced past Dan into the room. He nodded, relieved to see no sign of Dan and Wes's parents. "Can we talk?"

Dan's eyes narrowed, and he didn't budge from blocking the entrance to the room. "Why?"

"I'd like to discuss what happened this morning. That is, if you still want to marry my sister." He stared at the redness on Dan's cheek. "It looks like she had a go at you."

Though his frown deepened, Dan drew a breath then stepped back, holding the door open for Clark. His lips lifted in a sneer. "Just keep your hands off me. You already had my brother."

Way to start a conversation, asshole. Clark sucked in a calming breath and stepped into the room. He strode straight to the chair next to a small desk and sat. With his gaze locked on Dan, who stood with his hands fisted at his sides, Clark lowered his voice. "Let's get one thing very clear. I have *zero* interest in a narrow-minded jerk like you. *Zero.* A handshake is about the only touching I'm willing to do, but after your behavior, I'm good with skipping even that."

The former groom sagged a little, the angry sneer falling into a miserable frown.

Pointing a finger at Dan, Clark glared as he continued. "Regarding your brother, he and I had already arranged for him to stay over before we went out last night. So, in answer to your earlier question, no, we didn't get him drunk and date-rape him."

Dan held up his hands. "Look, dude, your sister and Wes both ripped me a new one already. So, if all you came here for was to yell at me, just go." Dan turned away and crossed his arms over his chest.

"I know they were here," Clark continued, schooling the anger in his voice. "I had to convince Wes to help sort this out, and I've already seen Grace. Right now, Wes is trying to catch her before our parents find out what you said, and before she tells them she called off the wedding."

Dan cringed but said nothing.

Clark leaned back in the chair. "I just want us to be clear before I help you."

Moving to the bed, Dan sat on the edge and stared at him, his expression full of misery. "Why would you want to help me? Your boyfriend almost punched me, and I accused you of rape."

"Look, you've been a real dick all of the times we've been forced together. I don't know what your specific problem with me is, though I get it. You hate gay people."

Dan's face reddened to match where Grace had slapped him. "I don't hate anyone," he mumbled.

Crossing his arms over his chest, Clark hardened his glare. "Could've fooled me."

Leaning forward, Dan rested his head in his hands. "Grace warned me about this weekend. I just can't stop my mouth sometimes. A lot of it is shit my dad said when I was growing up." He met Clark's gaze. "I know you're a nice guy. I can see it every time we're in the same room."

With a shake of his head, Clark huffed out a breath. "If I'm going to have to vouch for you with my whole family, you need to figure out how to treat me better."

"I don't know what to do, man." Dan's glance fled to the window. "It's so ingrained in me."

"Just be civil," Clark replied, exasperated he even needed to have this conversation. "Like I said, we can skip the handshake if it makes you that uncomfortable. Just can the abusive language."

He winced at Clark's words and turned back. "I'm…uh…sorry for what I said, and I'm going to try to be better." His eyebrows drew closer. "Not just for you and Grace, but for Wes, too."

Clark allowed a tight-lipped smile to form on his lips. "That's a start."

Dan let out a heavy sigh. "I don't know what else I can do, Clark. It was such a fucking shock. I didn't know…"

Not wavering in his gaze, Clark went to bat for Wes. "Your parents. You'll need to stand up to them if they make some nasty comment, or if they attack your brother. Keeping your mouth shut is one thing, but letting others denigrate someone you claim to love, even if it's your parents, makes you complicit."

"I'll try, man, but you've seen my mom." He gave a small shiver. "She's pretty fierce."

Clark frowned. "She's got nothing on Grace. Actions speak louder than words. You'll need to prove yourself to both people you claim to love."

Dan gripped the comforter. "I *do* love them," he said, heat returning to Dan's words.

Unfazed, Clark didn't flinch. "Prove it."

Dan sat silent for a few moments processing Clark's ultimatum. Clark sat patiently, hoping the man actually had a backbone.

With a solemn nod, Dan stood. "Yeah, okay. I'll jump all over them if they try to hurt Wes, and if they say anymore shit about you."

"Okay. Think about what you'll say, so you're not

stuck for words when the time comes." Clark rose. "Come on, let's go to my room. If Wes can convince Grace to work this out with you, he'll bring her there." He set his mouth into a smirk. "Just try to keep your hands off me and my date."

Shaking his head, Dan led the way to the door. "Not a problem, dude."

WES FOUND GRACE stalking down the third-floor hallway toward his parents' room. With some relief, he realized she hadn't had time to out him to his family. "Grace, wait."

She whipped around and glared before her face softened. "Wes? What are you doing here?"

He almost choked on the words. "I came to talk to you before you do something you'll regret."

She arched an eyebrow as he approached her. Her deep blue eyes glittered with righteous anger. "Regret? Are you kidding me?"

"Clark told me you called things off because of what happened this morning." He took in her appearance. Instead of a wedding dress and immaculate makeup, she wore jeans and had cleaned off her face. "Can we go somewhere and talk for a bit?"

Narrowing her eyes, she crossed her arms. "What would be the point? I told your brother we're through."

"Please, Grace. Just hear me out," he implored. Clark had said he'd have a hard time convincing her to change her mind. Still, he'd promised he'd try.

Not budging, she stood her ground. "We can talk

right here."

With a nervous glance at the door to his parents' room, he shook his head. "How about Clark and Mitch's room?" He lowered his voice. "I'd rather not discuss this in potential earshot of my mother."

She paused, glancing at the door, and seemed to reconsider. "Okay, Wes. I'll give you ten minutes." Her mouth tightened. "But I've already made up my mind."

With a sigh of relief, he stepped back to let her pass. "Thanks." He shared her anger and found himself at a loss for what to say. Falling into step behind her, he considered how he could change her mind.

Wes accompanied Grace to the elevator and pressed the button. He checked his watch. *Shit, it's already eleven.* Thinking through the events of the day, Wes should have been getting Dan into his suit about now. The wedding was at three. With Grace already out of most of her make-up, there wasn't much time to patch things up and get them dressed.

The doors opened a moment later, and they entered. He pressed the button for the fifth floor and turned to Grace, beginning with the obvious. "I know my brother can be a real dick."

She crossed her arms again with a huff. "That's for sure." Furrowing her brow, she narrowed her gaze. "Why are you trying to help him? He was horrible to you, my brother, and my brother's date."

The elevator dinged and came to a halt. Wes waited to answer until the doors opened and the coast was clear. Only empty hallway stretched out before them. "*Because* he's my brother. In his own messed up way, he was trying to look out for me. Unfortunately, he's the younger brother and hasn't quite mastered making things be about someone other than himself."

They followed the hallway until they reached Clark and Mitch's room. Wes tapped his fingers against the side of his leg, trying to figure out the best way to discuss Dan. He pulled the keycard from his pocket and opened the door.

Grace arched a sculpted eyebrow, a mischievous smirk temporarily replacing her angry scowl. "You have a key to their room?"

Heat burned across his face. "I, uh, told your fiancé to fuck off and moved into your brother's room."

"I see," she held her smirk for a moment then tightened her lips into a thin line as she stepped inside. "And yet, you want me to take his sorry ass back."

"I want you both happy." He followed, allowing the door to close behind them. "So, yeah."

Settling into the desk chair, she crossed her legs and her arms. "Why?"

He perched on the corner of the bed. "You fell in love with him for a reason. What was it?"

She furrowed her brow, stopping for a moment to consider. "I thought he was kind." A small smile crept across her lips. "He made me laugh, and he's very generous with his friends." The smile evaporated, and she leaned forward, uncrossing her arms to grip the armrests. "But I made it clear to him that my brother loves whoever he wants to, and I wouldn't tolerate any frat-boy bullshit."

"He didn't learn that behavior in the frat house," Wes said with an inward cringe. "I met several of his frat brothers yesterday, and they're decent guys. Most of them can't figure out where the homophobia came from." He shook his head. "None of them had met my parents."

"It doesn't matter where he learned it," she said, her voice rising. "The point is, I threatened to call off the wedding and dump his ass if he said or did anything shitty to Clark this weekend. He did. So, I did." She leaned back, leveling a stubborn stare at him. "I don't make idle threats."

Guilt burned through him. He slipped off the bed and knelt in front of her. "I won't pretend he didn't piss me the hell off this morning. But he got blind-sided, and it's my fault. I didn't intend for him to figure out I'm gay by finding me naked with his fiancée's brother."

Grace glared downward. "The fact he accused someone in my family of rape says all I need to know about him."

Wes's phone buzzed, and he fished it from his pocket. *Mission accomplished. We're on our way.* Relief washed over him, and he returned the phone to his pocket, refocusing his attention on Grace. "Do you really mean that? Damned by hasty words said in shock? Is there nothing redeemable about him?"

"Seriously?" Her fists clenched, and her nostrils flared.

"Please, Grace. Just hear me out." He paused, searching for something to say that wouldn't inflame her further. "What if Clark and Dan walked through that door right now having made their peace? Would you reconsider your decision?"

Considering, she paused, and her fists unclenched. She sat back in the chair, her face screwed up in thought. She raised her index finger. "*If* he makes his peace with Clark, *if* he accepts you being gay, and *if* he apologizes to you, Clark, and Mitch—to everyone's satisfaction—I'll consider going through with marrying him."

"Shake on it?" Wes said, rising and extending his hand.

Her gaze went from his hand to his face, and her brow furrowed suspiciously. "Why?"

Wes felt no guilt about setting her up. He knew he was doing the right thing. "Why hesitate? I think you're just trying to appease me," Wes pressed.

With reluctance, she reached out and took his hand. "I don't say anything I don't mean." With a firm shake, she withdrew her hand. "Besides, there's no way he'd get anywhere near Clark."

The beep of the lock caught their attention. Wes turned to the door, his heartbeat racing, and watched the door slowly swing open.

Staring at the floor, Dan shuffled into the room. "Um, hi Grace."

GRACE'S NOSTRILS FLARED again, and she rose from the desk chair. "Why do I get the feeling I've been set up?"

Striding across the room, Clark stood in front of his sister and shrugged. "Maybe you were, a little. But give this a chance. I don't want you to make a mistake because of me."

She glared at Dan before returning her attention to Clark. "It wasn't completely because of you or Wes. After that disastrous dinner his parents threw to get to know my family, I told that jackass over there," she said, pointing at Dan, "that I wouldn't put up with the religious bullshit his mom was spouting."

"You know, Grace, he did call her out." Clark held her glare. "You need to at least give him some credit for that."

Taking a breath, she stared down all four men before shifting her glare to Dan. "The point is, I warned you, Daniel Palucinski, and I follow through with my threats."

"I know." Dan stared at the floor again then slowly raised his head to look directly at his fiancée. "I fucked up. Majorly. This stuff's ingrained in me, and it's hard to change. But I want to."

She crossed her arms and huffed, her glare never wavering. "Pretty words."

Clark shook his head. "Geez, you're stubborn. He's already apologized to me and to Mitch."

With a chuckle, Mitch nodded. "I even agreed not to sock him in the jaw."

Wes whistled, not looking at Dan. "That's progress. The apology must have been pretty good."

A grin stretched Mitch's lips. "Definite progress."

Clark recognized the dour expression on Grace's face. She still wasn't satisfied, and she wasn't about to make it easy on Dan. Her gaze flicked between the two brothers. "Fine." She leaned forward, anger still sparking in her blue eyes. "But what about Wes?"

BRENT ARCHER

Dan's face burned bright red, much like Wes's did when Clark saw him flustered.

Wes crossed his arms, matching Grace's folded arms, and waited with a frown. Clark thanked his lucky stars he wasn't the one facing the formidable duo.

Taking a hesitant step forward, Dan's gaze dropped to the floor again. "I'm sorry, Wesley." He shook a little before bringing his gaze back up to meet his brother's glare.

The strange urge to hug Dan tugged at Clark as he watched the confident, straight boy turn into an emotional puddle.

Clearing his throat, Dan's eyes watered.

Grace wasn't so moved. "That's it?"

Dan stiffened. "I'm so sorry I wasn't there for you, bro," Dan said in a rush. The floodgates opened, and he spoke quickly. "I want to know more about your life, and if you want to tell Mom and Dad, I'll stand right beside you." His lip trembled, and he paused. "I love you, man. Don't ever think I don't."

Wes dropped his arms and stepped face to face with Dan, still frowning. "It's nice you actually want to be my brother again." He paused, searching Dan's face for a moment before nodding. "Okay. Let's see how this goes." He cast a quick glance at Clark and Mitch. "I have a lot to tell you."

Heat rose in Clark's face, and he contemplated telling Grace about Mitch. He'd probably have to fess up eventually if he wanted to ask Wes out on a date. But maybe not right now.

134

After giving Dan a hug, Wes kept an arm slung across his brother's shoulders. Together, they turned to face Grace. "That's your three conditions met, I think."

She pursed her lips, and for a moment, Clark was afraid she'd stick to her guns.

Wes arched his eyebrow. "You did shake on our agreement."

Standing, she approached Dan while Wes stepped away. She gently lay her hand on his cheek and brushed her thumb across the scratches. "I slapped you pretty hard, didn't I?"

He drew a deep, shaky breath. "Yeah, but I deserved it."

She surveyed his face. "I have some cover-up that'll take care of the redness."

Clark stiffened. No way would homophobic Dan ever agree to wear make-up.

Taking a deep breath, Dan nodded. "Okay."

"Holy shit," Wes muttered.

After an arch of his eyebrow at his brother, Dan turned his focus back onto Grace. "I'll never give you reason to get that angry with me again." He placed his hands on her hips. "I love you, Grace. Please, I don't want to lose you."

"I'm not usually violent, I swear." She stared deep into his eyes. "It's how I react when someone threatens Clark."

Heat spread through Clark's cheeks. His mind flashed briefly on the crying bully Grace took down when he was a teenager. He knew she meant every word.

Wes backed away from his brother and joined Clark.

He bent toward Clark's ear and whispered, "I think we just saved Christmas."

With a shake of his head, Clark whispered back, "She still hasn't actually said she'll marry him." Until she said the words, he knew they weren't out of the woods yet.

Grace turned to face the three of men, a frown still on her face but her anger clearly dissipated. "Okay, boys, your little plan has worked—as long as you all agree to one last condition."

With a frown of his own, Clark glanced around at the other men. "And that is?"

She pointed to her brother. "Clark is now one of the groomsmen." She swung her pointing finger to Wes. "And he stands next to Wes." The gleam in her eye was unmistakable. "No offense, Mitch?"

Mitch grinned. "None taken." He winked at Clark.

CHAPTER NINE

WES STOOD NEXT to his brother as they waited at the altar with the minister, *Pachelbel's Canon* grating on his nerves. His mother had insisted on it, and Dan had to cave to keep the peace. Wes thought back to Grace's condition, and if it had been him, he'd have insisted on changing the music. None of the wedding party would have objected.

The wedding party processed with Clark leading the way next to the maid of honor. He chuckled to himself to see his mother's hackles go up the moment she spied Clark, and he exchanged a glance with Dan. His brother winked and grinned.

Warmth spread through Wes when Clark took his place next to him. He leaned over and whispered in Clark's ear. "What do you think Mitch has in mind for us tonight?"

A smile lit up Clark's face. "I don't know, but I bet it'll be memorable." He nodded toward Wes's mother. "I think she's about to launch out of her seat to defend her little boy's virtue from the big bad gay."

Wes glanced at his mother's face, which had hardened into an angry glare at Clark. He dropped his glance to

Clark. "I could really mess with her by kissing you on the cheek right now." He wanted to kiss Clark in front of everyone so badly. It would certainly take care of coming out to his family.

"We've had enough drama for one wedding," Clark murmured. "Save it for tonight."

The wedding march filled the room, and the guests stood. Nearly all gazes were on Grace's entrance with her father. Wes's mother, however, ignored the bride and locked her hawkish gaze on him. A frown creased her makeup, and she emphatically shook her head.

Wes met her glare with one of his own, mouthing the word *behave*.

Her eyes widened, shock clearly washing over her. She whipped her head around to stare at Grace.

Dan gave him a little nudge. "Nice one, bro."

With a quick glance at his brother, Wes grinned. "Thanks."

Grace climbed the steps, and her dad stepped back. Dan moved forward and shook the older man's hand. "I'll make you proud of me, sir. Thanks for allowing me to marry your daughter."

Raising an eyebrow, Mr. Adamson's face betrayed some skepticism, but he nodded and gave Dan a pat on the shoulder. "I hope so." He found his seat, and Dan and Grace turned and gave Reverend Randy their full attention.

The ceremony went off beautifully, and the kiss between Dan and Grace lingered to the hoots and cheers of their gathered friends and family. Wes wondered if he'd ever find someone to kiss like that in front of a roomful of loved ones. He glanced at Clark and was rewarded with a nod and a grin. *Yeah, I think I already have.* His resolve strengthened, and he glanced at his mother. She applauded with the rest of the wedding guests, but her gaze flashed to first Wes then Clark.

American Author's *Best Day of My Life* blared through the room, and the guests shot to their feet, cheering. Dan and Grace, both with big smiles on their faces, danced down the aisle. Noting his mother's mounting fury at the recessional song she *clearly* had not picked, Wes chuckled and followed, busting a move with the maid of honor until they reached the back of the church. Clark grooved out while escorting one of the bridesmaids.

Grace gave each of the wedding party a hug as they emerged from the sanctuary. When Wes reached her, she gave him a squeeze and whispered, "Clark's quite a catch," into his ear.

Heat rose up from his toes to the top of his head. She released him and moved on to her brother. By the reaction Clark had, eyes bulging and spluttering to say something, her words to him must have held a similar theme.

Directing the groomsmen to one side of the bride and groom and the bridesmaids to the other, Grace ensured that Clark and Wes stood together. Wes chuckled to himself at her obvious match-making. Not that he minded. Clark looked stunning in his tux.

Watching both sets of parents moving into the foyer, Clark leaned toward Wes. "Do you think Grace figured out Mitch?"

Before Wes could answer, his mother approached. "Wesley, dear, I need you to go fetch my shawl from my room." Her words were directed toward her son, but her sneer was aimed at Clark.

Dan stepped forward with a frown on his face. "No. If you're cold, Mother, Dad can wrap his arm around you or give you his jacket. Wes is staying right here." He gave her a stern glare. "Next to Clark."

She stiffened her back and raised her chin.

Wes braced for her nasty retort, but Dan took her arm before she could say a word and drew her to the side. "We've already had enough of your bullshit with the music you forced down our throats for *our* ceremony," he said angrily, under his breath. "If you don't back off from Wes and Clark right now, I'll make sure you *never* see your grandchildren."

Wes clamped his jaw shut, realizing the bomb had dropped. He'd never seen Dan be this forceful with their mother.

Clearly at a loss for words, his mom tightened her lips and accompanied her son to stand with her husband at the end of the line of bridesmaids.

Grace, clearly swooning at the display of Dan's new backbone, stepped closer to Wes and Clark. "I knew he had it in him."

Clark's parents approached, and each gave their daughter a hug.

"You look so beautiful, honey," her mother said. Mrs. Adamson turned her attention onto Wes. "You look very handsome, Wesley." Her mouth curved in a knowing smile. "And I see you're becoming well-acquainted with our Clark." She patted his cheek. "Just be sure not to steal him away from Mitch."

More heat swelled through Wes, and he spluttered to respond. Mrs. Adamson hadn't been fooled by his straight persona. Obviously, this reception was going to be all about making him blush.

Clark came to his rescue. "Now, Mom. Mitch and I are, uh…" he glanced at Wes. "Just friends. He agreed to come here with me, but we're not officially dating or anything."

Stifling a laugh at the technically correct explanation, Wes nodded. "I know Mitch, too, and I was relieved to find out they weren't an item." He gave Clark a glance of his own. "I hope to see Clark a lot more often, now that we're family."

She laid a hand on his shoulder. "I would hope so. You two boys should come to dinner when we're all back in Seattle. Invite Mitch, too." She turned to look at the wedding guests moving down the reception line. "Oh dear, I'd better get into my place. Come on, Harvey."

Escorting his wife away, Mr. Adamson shot them a grin. "Yes, dear."

Dan returned to take his place next to Wes, and Grace leaned around her husband. "I swear I didn't say a word." She didn't even try to hide her excitement.

Clearly, Wes wasn't fooling anyone. No wonder his mother was being so nasty to Clark. Wes shrugged. "Don't worry, Grace. I don't care who knows anymore."

The long line of Grace and Dan's friends filed past,

and Wes kept his tone pleasant, smiling and greeting everyone who stopped to shake his hand and chat.

Claire stopped in front of Clark. "Such a handsome young man." She winked at Wes. "Are you two dating?"

"Oh-my-God, Auntie." Clark's face whitened.

Wes shook her hand. "Not at the moment, ma'am, but I plan to ask him to dinner when we get back to Seattle."

"Oh, good." She leaned in to give him a peck on the cheek. "He's a hunk."

His face still drawn, Clark turned to Wes after she moved on. "Sorry, Wes. I swear I didn't prompt her or anything." He narrowed his eyes and glanced at Grace. "Maybe my *dear* sister…"

Sparing him a quick glance, Grace smirked at them then returned her attention to Claire.

Claire's son Duncan stepped forward next. "Nice to see you again. Wes, right?" He shook Wes's hand. "Sorry about that Amy dance last night. I felt pretty bad for you."

Dan whipped his head around. "Dude, what?"

Chuckling, Duncan moved along to stand in front of him. "You've got to know how uncomfortable the poor guy was."

With a meaningful look at Wes, Dan nodded his understanding. "I didn't then, but I do now."

Before he could say anything else, Leif stood in front of Clark grinning. "Yeah, I thought the poor guy was going to heave."

Wes hung his head for a second. The heat of his embarrassment surged up his neck and bloomed across his cheeks. "Not a fun way to spend the bachelor's party."

"Don't worry," Dan said and patted him on the shoulder. "I'll get the right stripper for your party, bro."

Rolling his eyes, Wes focused on Clark's cousin. "Hi, Leif, nice to see you again."

"Likewise." Leif tilted his head toward the people behind him. "I think your stripper is about four people behind me."

Glancing to his left, Wes didn't have to count to see Leif meant Mitch. The escort schmoozed his way through the line of the wedding party, and Wes turned back to Leif. He could have denied his interest in the tall, red-head, but instead, he gave a wry smile. "No objection here. Clark?"

Snickering, Clark shrugged. "You'd have to see how much he charges to take his clothes off." He winked at Wes.

Leif and Duncan roared with laughter, likely because they thought Wes might be embarrassed. Wes shot Clark a frown, shocked he'd even bring up the escort part of Mitch's role for the weekend. Not that anyone but Clark would know.

Turning toward them, Grace's face lit up with mischief. "I'd pay to see that."

Clark pulled a face. "Too bad he's not interested in *girls*."

"Besides," Dan threw in. "You've got a prime stud right here." He used his thumbs to point to himself.

Claire giggled, and Clark's cousins bellowed out another laugh.

Before he lost complete control of this situation, Wes ignored his new sister-in-law and returned his attention to Leif. "We'll make sure you're invited to put out any fires that flare up."

It was Leif's turn to blush furiously. Worry lit his eyes briefly before a grin reappeared. "We'll have to see." He gave Clark a quick hug.

"Did you want to ask me something, cuz?" Clark asked after they'd separated.

Leif bit his lip and shook his head. "Not here…" His face brightened. "Congratulations on your two new brothers."

Wes pondered the strange reaction but put Leif out of his mind when the next guest stood in front of him.

Mitch made his way along the line of groomsmen and gave Wes a wink. "How are you holding up?"

"Okay," Wes replied. Leif, Duncan, and Dan's conversation had him flustered, heat both flashing across his face and threatening to stir the raging beast of his cock.

"I saw the interaction with your mother while you and Dan were waiting for Grace's entrance." He grinned. "Nice one."

Wes glanced down the line at his parents. Though they both wore pleasant masks, pretending to be reasonable people while talking to a pair of Grace's sorority sisters, Wes could see his mother's fury simmering just under the surface. Her back was a little too stiff. Bright red blotches of color filled her cheeks. He turned back to Mitch. "There's going to be hell to pay later."

Mitch took his hand to shake, but also swiped his

finger along the underside of Wes's wrist. "Just remember what's coming after the reception." With a leer, he moved on to Dan.

Another fiery blush worked its way up Wes's neck, the heat reaching his face. Once the guests had all filed past, Wes summoned up his courage and pulled Dan aside while Grace hugged one of her bridesmaids. "Dan, I need a minute with you."

A shadow crossed his brother's face, and his brow furrowed. "We're okay, right, bro? I was just kidding about the stripper."

"Yeah, we're good. Don't worry." He shot a furtive look at their parents standing near the entrance of the room by themselves. "I think I need to tell Mom and Dad that I'm gay. I'm pretty sure the cat's already out of the bag, but I don't want this blowing up in front of your guests."

Dan nodded, unfazed by his declaration. "Want me there with you?"

Unsure what to make of Dan's offer, Wes hesitated. "Do you really *want* to be there when the shit hits the fan?"

Placing his hands on Wes's shoulders, Dan nodded again. "I made you a promise I'd be better. Let me prove it, bro."

Gratitude and relief flowed through him. "Okay. I could use the support." He glanced at their parents again. His mother's scowl darkened that corner of the room, and the rest of the wedding party steered clear of the pair.

"You want to do it now? I'm sure Grace will wait for

us to make our entrance." Dan eagerly motioned for Grace to come over.

She giggled at something her maid of honor said and hurried across the room to them. "Sorry, Carly was just saying how hot you and Clark are." She grinned. "I told her you were both spoken for."

With a nervous chuckle, Wes glanced at his brother.

Before he could speak, Dan addressed his wife. "Wes is going to come out to Mom and Dad. Do you mind if we get it over with before we go into the reception hall?" He bit his bottom lip then turned back to Wes. "Sorry, bro. Hope that was okay to say."

Grace crossed her arms, her brow furrowed. "You're going with him, right?" She fixed Dan with a stern glare, the warning in her question clear.

Wes's love for his new sister-in-law grew leaps and bounds. Grace not only approved and was willing to hold up the whole production for Wes's moment, but she was also pushing her husband to go into battle with him as backup.

"That sums it up." Wes leaned forward and gave her a kiss on the cheek. "Thanks, Grace. This shouldn't take long."

She hugged him. "Good luck." Smiling at her husband, she kissed him. "I'm proud of you." Wes caught the word that left her mouth as she turned away. "Grandkids."

Their parents stood together off to the side of the main group, waiting to go into the reception hall. Wes's stomach did somersaults as the two brothers crossed the room and approached the imposing couple.

Wes could have hoped for more privacy for this moment, but his mother's stubborn stance said there'd be no moving her.

Crossing her arms, their mother glared at Dan. "I assume you've come to apologize for how you spoke to me."

Dan gave a single shake of his head. "Nope."

Her eyes widened, the blotches on her face deepening.

"Actually," Wes said, stepping forward. "I have something to tell you."

She pursed her lips but said nothing.

"You've probably noticed I've been spending a lot of time this weekend with Grace's brother Clark." Wes paused, unsure if his nerve would hold out.

She hissed in a breath. "That little fa—"

Dan took an aggressive step forward and pinned his mother with his glare. "Don't you *ever* use that word again."

Their father puffed up his chest. "How dare you. I didn't raise you to speak to your mother like that."

Meeting the glare head on, Dan faced off with their dad. "No, you taught me to hate people different from me, and it almost cost me Grace *and* Wesley. I don't know what your problem with gay people is, but if you keep on with your hate-filled bullshit, you'll never see any kids Grace and I have."

The redness creeping up his father's face made Wes worry the man might have heart attack. He spluttered, his mouth gaping and closing.

Dan cut him off before he could speak. "Now, Wes

has something to say to you both, and you'll listen." He turned to his brother. "Go for it, bro. I've got your back."

Amazed at this new and supportive Dan, Wes turned to his mother. He steeled his courage. "I'm gay." With just two words, his shoulders lightened immediately, and the terror he'd felt since he was a kid melted away. Free of his secret and his need to hide who he was, he breathed a happy sigh. "I'm gay, and I'm going to ask Clark out."

To her credit, his mother didn't scream. Her disappointed stare spoke volumes, and she sighed heavily, the corners of her mouth turning downward in defeat.

His father stood in shocked silence, his face reddening further. Disgust, disbelief, and rage swirled across his face.

The lack of acceptance or love from his dad's reactions stung deeply, but Wes had expected nothing less from the man who cared more about other people's perceptions than the emotional well-being of his children.

Regaining her voice, his mother stared, eyes wet and on the verge of tears. "I know what you are," she whispered. "I've dreaded this day since you were in high school."

"It wasn't my choice, Mom." He glanced at Clark chatting happily with his sister. "And I've fallen hard for someone."

"Clark," she spat. The word dripped with anger and hatred. "I knew he'd pull you away from the right path."

Wes stiffened. "If you mean accepting who I am and being happy, I made that choice long before I met Clark." He turned to Dan, the urge to come clean about a few things almost overwhelming. "None of those girls I named when you asked me about a date for the wedding were real. Sorry I lied."

Dan shrugged. "I know, bro. Doesn't matter. I was a shit, and I know it." He glanced at their parents before returning his attention to Wes. "I'm gonna make it up to you."

Grinning, Wes gave his brother a hug. "Thanks, Dan."

Once they pulled back from their embrace, their father finally found his voice. "Wesley, you've made your choice. Don't expect any support from us."

Wes focused his attention on his father. Though hurt and disappointed, he held his head high. "You haven't been there for me for years, and I didn't expect you to suddenly change now. I fully accept you and Mom not wanting me around. After today, I won't burden you with my presence." He turned and strode across the room. He had no interest in whatever else they had to say.

Dan caught up with him before he got halfway across the room. "Hey, are you okay?"

Wes nodded. "I'm all right. Let's go and celebrate your big day, little brother."

With a grin, Dan waved Grace over. "I love you, bro."

AS THE PARTY wound down, and after Grace and Dan said their goodnights to a chorus of catcalls and loud cheering, Clark sidled up next to Mitch.

His date wrapped a beefy arm around his waist and grinned. "Hey, sexy. Where did you go?"

"The gangbang in the men's room with Dan's frat

brothers distracted me." Clark made an exaggerated display of wiping his mouth with his hand.

Mitch chuckled. "You won't mind, then, if I fuck the daylights out of Wesley while you watch from the couch, right?"

"Let's not be hasty," Clark retorted, flaring his nostrils in alarm. "I was actually wishing Aunt Claire and her boys goodnight. It's weird. I get the feeling like Leif wants to say something to me, but he keeps shrugging whatever it is off."

"He probably wants to tell you something about himself," Mitch said with a gleam in his eyes.

Clark widened his own. "Wait!" He leaned in closer and lowered his voice. "You're not working for him as well, are you?"

With a bark of laughter, Mitch shook his head. "Nope. Though he *is* smokin' hot. There must be something in the water with your family. Because, damn…" He leaned back, eyeing Clark's butt.

Wes approached, a drink in his hand. He arched one eyebrow at Mitch. "Clark sure does have a mighty fine ass. Don't you agree?"

Mitch nodded. "Mighty."

Ready to change the subject, Clark quirked an eyebrow at Wes. "Your folks were pretty quiet during dinner. Everything okay?" Not that he really cared about the Palucinskis being comfortable, but he'd noticed Mrs. Palucinski averting her eyes every time anyone from Clark's family approached her.

"Don't really care," Wes said with a shrug. "I told my

folks. Officially, I mean."

With a gasp, Clark's mouth dropped. "What? When did you do that?"

With a smile Clark nearly swooned over, Wes took a quick sip of his drink. "Right before Grace and Dan made their entrance at the reception."

Mitch stared at him, equally shocked. "And how did that go?"

"Well, Mom didn't scream, and that's a win." Wes gave another shrug. "I probably won't have to deal with her or Dad for a long time, though you might get some glares at breakfast if they bother to show. Dan was right there with me and read her the riot act. He meant it about the grandkids."

Clark scanned the room for Grace's mother-in-law but didn't see either of the Palucinskis. "Are you all right?"

"Just fine." Wes smiled. "I'm finally able to be who I am, and Dan's already turning into a better brother than he's ever been. I owe you both some major thanks."

Looking around the ballroom, Clark noticed several of the guests drifting away toward the exits. A group of Grace's sorority sisters were doing shots with a few of Dan's frat brothers.

Wes laughed, following Clark's gaze. "I guess we're not the only ones getting lucky tonight."

With a chuckle of his own, Mitch nudged Clark. "It's amazing those guys have the energy to go for round two."

Clark huffed, feigning outrage. "Are you implying I couldn't satisfy a group of frat boys?"

Wes's eyes bugged. "What?"

Kissing his temple, Mitch wrapped his arm around Clark's waist. "It's amazing all those guys could fit in that bathroom."

Clark laughed, wriggling his eyebrows. "It was a tight fit."

Mitch gave Clark's ass a squeeze. "I know."

Wes shook his head, a blush creeping up his neck and across his cheeks. "You hooked up with Dan's frat brothers?" He glanced again at the gaggle of frat boys and sorority girls.

Before Clark could respond, Mitch piped up. "That's why he's walking funny."

Puffing out a breath, Clark narrowed his eyes at the escort. "I'm not *that* much of a slut." He turned to Wes. "No frat boys were deflowered in the course of this joke."

"Thank goodness for that," Wes breathed. "The last thing this wedding needs is more drama, remember?" He downed the rest of his drink. "I've only had two of these, plus the champagne, and several glasses of water."

Mitch nodded approvingly. "Good boy. I wouldn't want you passing out before the fun really begins, even though you really deserve the drinks for coming out."

Curiosity seized Clark, and he stared at his date. "So, what was this reward you mentioned for saving the wedding?"

A smirk inched across Mitch's lips, and he clapped and rubbed his hands together. "If you're ready, let's go back to our room, and you'll find out."

"Wait here. I'll be right back." Wes strode across the room toward the bar.

Mitch stared after their companion. "What do you suppose he's up to?"

With a shrug, Clark watched Wes's progress, admiring the way he filled out his slacks. A sweet guy, a sweet ass, and finally and completely out of the closet. Wes Palucinski was the total package, and Clark's stomach tightened at the prospect of a date with Grace's new brother-in-law.

Pausing at the thought, Clark tore his gaze from Wes's ass. "Do you think it's wrong to date your sister's brother-in-law?"

Mitch chuckled, but Clark didn't miss the wistful smile. "No, I think it's fine. You two seem to have some chemistry."

With an appreciative rake of his gaze over Mitch, warmth spread through Clark's body anticipating the rest of their night together. "I think all three of us have good chemistry."

Nodding at the bartender, Wes returned with three champagne flutes, a small container of orange juice, and a bottle of champagne. A grin spread across his handsome face. "For tomorrow morning."

Clark returned the grin. "Let's go. I can't wait to get you two naked."

They hurried from the hotel's ballroom and caught the elevator to their floor. Clark led the way to the room, swiping his key in the lock and holding open the door for the other two men.

Wes set the bottles in the minibar fridge and the three glasses onto the desk while Mitch moved across the room to the bed. On the bedside table were two plastic bottles and a bouquet of dahlias. Several condom packages lay in front of the vase.

Eager to get things started, Clark shrugged off his tux jacket and tossed it onto the easy chair. "What's all this?"

"The flowers are for both of you," Mitch said. "My admiration for what you did for your brother and sister. The bottles are massage oil and lube." A smirk spread across his lips as he lifted one of the condom packages. "I'm sure this is self-explanatory."

Wes surveyed the table. "Massage oil?"

"I studied nine months at massage school and got my certification." Mitch rubbed his hands together. "You boys had a rough day, and part of your reward is a relaxing rubdown." He stared at the two men expectantly. "Who's first?"

Pulling his tux shirt away from the metal studs and loosening his cufflinks and tie, Clark let his shirt fall open. "I think Wes deserves the first massage. He came out today, and that's cause, all by itself, for celebration."

Wes's face reddened. "I'm happy to go first if you're okay with that." He opened the fly of his slacks and let the garment drop.

Motioning for Mitch to join him, Clark stepped in front of Wes and placed a hand on his cheek. "Let us undress you. You're so handsome."

Mitch quickly shed his clothes until he stood next to the two men in nothing but a pair of blue briefs with a slit up the back and a built-in pouch showcasing his impressive bulge.

Clark raked his gaze over the escort's magnificent physique, thanking his lucky stars he had two such amazing men sharing his bed this evening. He reached out a hand, rubbed the solid chest muscles, then tweaked a nipple. The bulge in Mitch's shorts quickly grew until the outline of his erection filled out the pouch and stretched the thin fabric.

With a low moan, Mitch grabbed Clark's hand before he could further exploit the sensitive nubs. "If you keep that up, you're going to miss out on your massage."

His own cock growing in his slacks, Clark contemplated skipping the sensual part of the evening. "I'm not seeing a downside here."

Chuckling and tugging the knot out of his bowtie, Wes unbuttoned his shirt and slipped it from his shoulders. "I do." He winked at Clark. "Don't worry. I'll make it worth your while to wait."

Clark hooked his fingers into the elastic of Wes's boxer-briefs and tugged them down. "Let's get started." Sinking to his knees, he sucked the hard, throbbing cock into his mouth.

"Oh, fuck," Wes moaned, his knees trembling.

Mitch moved to Wes's side and planted a kiss on his lips, while Clark glanced up and bobbed on the shaft, giving the head a swipe with his tongue on each upward thrust.

Pushing on Clark's shoulders as he broke the kiss with Mitch, Wes's whole body shook. "Massage," he gasped.

Mitch cracked his knuckles. "Get on the bed."

Wes hurried onto the sheets and lay on his stomach,

arching his back and pushing up his ass. He obviously knew what he wanted touched first.

Letting out a whistle, Clark's already rock-hard cock throbbed in his underwear. "Looks good enough to eat."

With a chuckle, Mitch climbed onto the bed and straddled Wes's hips. He tugged off the pouch of his sexy underwear and tossed it at Clark.

The musky fabric hit Clark's face before he could grab it. The scent of the escort filled his nostrils. He watched the erection surge out of the opening of the now front-less shorts and lay along the valley between Wes's pert ass cheeks.

"Clark, grab the massage oil and climb up here on the bed with me." Mitch nodded toward Wes. "We'll rub this boy down together."

Not needing to be asked twice, Clark kicked off his shoes, shrugged off his shirt, dropped his slacks and briefs, and tugged off his socks. He snatched the bottle from the bedside table and joined the two men on the bed.

Mitch chuckled. "I'm overdressed for this party." He reached for what remained of his underwear, but Clark stopped him.

"Not yet. I think it's sexy." He eyed the fabric framing Mitch's thickness, a flare of red hair peeking from the blue border.

"Okay," mitch purred in his deepest rumbly tone. "Drizzle some of the oil onto Wes's back."

With another pulse racing through his dick, Clark placed his knees on either side of Wes's head and leaned forward. He popped open the lid and did as Mitch instructed.

Wes sucked in a breath when the liquid hit his skin. The oil pooled along his spine and beaded down the sides of his ribs. Mitch placed a hand into the oil and rubbed along Wes's flanks. He spread the oil all over Wes's back and brought a hand to slick his own erection.

Each man drawing closer to the other, Mitch and Clark leaned forward and met halfway above Wes. Mitch tilted his head slightly to the left and pressed his lips together with Clark's. The contact sent fireworks shooting behind Clark's closed eyes, and Mitch's tongue slipped into his mouth.

Wes gripped Clark's thighs and raised his head to wrap his mouth over the cock in front of him. Warmth and a pleasurable suction made Clark moan into the kiss.

Breaking the lip-lock, Mitch moved his hands along Wes's back, causing the man beneath them to repeat Clark's moan. The vibration around Clark's hardness brought a tingling in his balls, and he pulled back, dislodging his dick from Wes's mouth.

With a glance into Clark's eyes, Wes rubbed his legs. "Something wrong?" His gaze dropped back to the sheet as Mitch ground his palms into Wes's shoulders. "Aaah…"

"I was just getting a little too excited." Clark let the sensation of imminent release pass before he got back in range of Wes's reach.

Mitch continued the massage, pressing his elbows into the pillows of Wes's ass. He gave each cheek a slap and sat back. "Roll over. I'll do your legs later."

Complying, Wes rolled onto his back. His cock

slapped against his abdomen, and he settled back, staring up into Clark's eyes. Every inch of Wes, from his dark, styled hair to his perfectly-shaped feet excited Clark. The large nipples on the moderately defined chest. The curly dusting of hair circling each pec and the dark trail leading to a trimmed patch just above his meaty cock. Large balls resting against thick, sturdy legs covered with the same dark hair.

"Switch places with me." Mitch scooted around the bed and nudged Clark to take his place between Wes's legs. He snagged the massage oil and rubbed some onto his hands before closing the lid and setting it back on the table. His fingers and palms pressed into Wes's chest, tracing the circle of his nipples and making the man gasp and arch his back.

Clark took the opportunity to grab Wes's cock and run his tongue around the head, darting at the slit in the top. Another moan accompanied a drop of clear fluid pushing from the tip. Sweet and salt danced on Clark's taste buds, and he pressed his lips around the head and began his downward journey.

Continuing his nipple work, Mitch scooted forward and aimed his formidable erection at Wes's gaping mouth. He slid the head inside, and Wes clamped his mouth around the shaft.

"That's it, Wes," Mitch crooned. "Let me fuck your mouth while Clark makes love to your cock."

Clark loved the sound of Mitch's sultry tones. He slid his oily fingers along the pucker of Wes's ass, nudging his legs wider. Inhaling, he slowly sucked in more of the throbbing, leaking erection while he pressed his index finger inside.

The opening clamped around Clark's finger, and Wes thrust his hips upward. The shaft inched deeper into Clark's throat, making him gag and forcing him to pull away from his prize. He kept his finger in its place, probing deeper and grazing against the hard nugget of Wes's prostate.

Wes lifted his head, allowing Mitch's cock to drop from his mouth. "Fuck, that's amazing."

Raising his hands from Wes's chest, Mitch leaned down and pressed their lips together. Clark gave the prostate another poke, generating a loud groan from Wes, partially muffled by Mitch's mouth.

Clark took a moment to admire the two exceptional men before him. Mitch's fiery hair mingled with Wes's dark locks. Pulling back only for a moment, their gazed lock, and Clark could see the passion and emotion of their connection ramp up. Their lips met again, and a wave of something much stronger than lust washed over Clark. He sucked in a breath, taken aback by the intensity of the unexpected blast of emotion.

After one last peck of a kiss, Mitch sat back and brought his gaze to Clark. "Your turn."

With a shake of his head, Clark slowly withdrew his finger from Wes. "The only thing I want to massage right now is this." His voice shook slightly, but he gave Wes's ass a playful slap. Working the tight hole before him only swelled his desire to be buried deep inside Wes and to share the same connection he'd just witnessed with Mitch.

Without a word, Mitch grabbed a condom and tossed it to Clark. Then he snatched the lube and squirted a dollop onto his fingers. While Mitch leaned across Wes's body to slick his pucker and press a finger inside, Clark ripped open the package and rolled the rubber over his own dick.

Mitch's eyes bulged as he withdrew his fingers from Wes. "Oh, fuck yeah, Wes. Eat my hole."

Clark glanced over to see Mitch balancing on one hand and gasping, his legs spread. Wes had maneuvered around to bury his face between Mitch's spread cheeks. Shaking, Mitch wrapped his lubed hand around Clark's covered shaft and stroked.

The gazes met, and Clark got lost in the intense desire reflecting back at him from Mitch's beautiful blue eyes. His strong grip made Clark's cock throb and grow harder. Mitch sifted his gaze down and guided the head to Wes's waiting pucker.

A muffled moan from Wes still rimming Mitch's ass accompanied Clark's entry. A velvety pressure wrapped around his shaft, setting off little earthquakes throughout Clark's body. His cock was a perfect fit inside Wes.

Clark reveled in the sensations of each thrust. Wes ground his ass in time to the gentle rhythm Clark established. Mitch moved off Wes's face and shucked his skimpy underwear. He tossed the briefs away and pulled Clark into a scorching kiss.

Increasing the intensity of his fucking to match Mitch's thrusting tongue, Clark pounded hard. Wes wrapped his legs around Clark's waist and urged him deeper. When the tingle began again, Clark ended the kiss with Mitch and untangled himself from Wes's legs, his cock still planted deep but not moving.

Panting from the pounding, Wes arched an eyebrow. "Getting close?"

Clark nodded, unable to speak a word.

"I want you next, Mitch." With a moan, Wes pulled his knees to his chest. "Show me you still want to be in me."

Reluctant to pull away from Wes, but needing to take a break so he wouldn't come too soon, Clark eased out and moved aside as Mitch grabbed a condom and took his place. The escort ripped the package open, tossed the foil to the side, and rolled the rubber down his shaft. He slid his thickness where Clark had just been.

"Yeah, Wesley, Clark opened you up perfectly." Mitch continued driving forward until his hips pressed against Wes's ass. Leaning down, Mitch kissed the whimpering man deeply.

After tugging the condom off, Clark tossed it to the floor. Wes reached for him, and he moved in next to the two men. Mitch set a slow stirring rhythm, and Clark closed in for a kiss.

Warmth flooded through Clark when their lips touched. Mitch wrapped him in an embrace and pulled him closer as their lip-lock intensified. Tongues dueled and swiped at each other. Clark pulled back for a moment, losing himself in the icy blue of Wes's eyes.

The embrace slackened, and Wes drew a hand up to caress Clark's cheek, whispering, "I want you."

A welling of emotion pushed Clark to return to the kiss, surpassing the intensity of before. This wasn't going to be a one-time thing with Wes. He broke the kiss and trailed his lips along Wes's jawline and down his neck. A salty taste danced on his tongue as he lapped at the sweat-slicked skin.

Loud moans filled the room as Wes writhed under both men. "Oh, my God, Clark. I want you inside me again. Please."

Pulling himself up, Clark scooted to the edge of the bed. Mitch increased his rhythm to a steady pounding. Clark slipped on another condom and lubed his cock. Mitch's pert ass just barely dusted with hair rising and sinking in front of him made his dick pulse, as did the sight of Wes's head resting on the pillow, with his mouth hanging open and his eyes rolled back while Mitch pounded him.

Deciding he wanted to fuck them both at the same time, Clark laced his fingers into the red hair in front of him and gently tugged Mitch's head back. After lining up his cock against Mitch's pucker, tight warmth gripped the shaft and pulled him inside. The combined pressure and motion threatened to quickly stroke his load out of him.

With a shudder, the escort moaned. "I'm not going to last long sandwiched between you two."

"Not a problem." Clark thrust deep, pressing Mitch into Wes. Both men cried out, and Wes opened his legs wider apart to accommodate Mitch.

Setting a fast pace, Clark slammed in and out of Mitch, grinding him deep into Wes. The tingle in his balls grew in intensity the longer he continued his drilling.

"Fuck!" Mitch flung back his head against Clark's shoulder and bellowed out his orgasm.

Clark gave a deep thrust and held still, the convulsing muscles clamping around his cock pulling him over the edge. He reached around and gripped Mitch's chest, holding tight, and unloaded into the condom buried deep.

Clutching the sheet with one hand and pulling both Clark and Mitch tighter against him with his legs and feet, Wes shuddered as his hand flew over his hardness. He shouted out his release, shaking with each shot.

Clark eased himself out of Mitch, who let out a gasp once the head left his ass. Careful not to spill the contents of the full rubber, he eased it off his cock and tied it off.

A whimper came from Wes when Mitch pulled out and sat back. Wes wiped an arm across his sweaty brow and slowly sank onto the bed.

"Let me help you with that." Clark tugged the condom off the red-head's half-hard dick and marveled at the amount of white liquid filling half the rubber.

Wes let out a whistle. "I'm always amazed at how much you shoot."

With a chuckle, Mitch moved farther up the bed, and his head hit the pillow. "That was incredible, guys."

"Definitely." Clark slipped off the bed with the two condoms and stepped over their abandoned clothes into the bathroom. A feeling of satisfaction washed over him as he tossed the rubbers into the trash and pulled a washcloth from the rack. He ran the warm water and wiped himself off. After rinsing the rag, he returned to the bed and ran the cloth over the escort's cock.

A sleepy smile spread across Mitch's face. "Thanks. You're such a gentleman." A flash of something Clark could only define as longing sparked in Mitch's eyes. Mitch reached up with one hand and drifted his fingers along Clark's cheek. "So beautiful." He let his fingertips ghost down Clark's neck and shoulder, leaving waves of tender pleasure in their wake.

Clark closed his eyes for a moment, savoring the sweetness of Mitch's touch. When the fingers left his skin, Clark sighed and turned to Wes. The dark-haired beauty stared up at him, a similar emotion playing across his face. Clark wiped off the mess from the dark chest hair and treasure trail. "You made quite a mess."

"It's probably because Mitch's massage got me so worked up." He winked up at Clark. "You stroking me while he worked my chest made it even better."

Clark tossed the washcloth on the floor. Mitch turned and spooned against Wes, sliding an arm over him. Joining the two men, Clark pulled the covers over them and faced Wes. His hand caressed along Wes's ribs and across Mitch's muscular arm.

A soft sigh came from Wes, and a gentle snore from Mitch.

Nestling between the two men, Wes settled his head on Clark's chest, the silky hair caressing his skin.

Clark kissed the top of Wes's head. "Guess we wore him out."

CHAPTER TEN

"MORNIN', BRO." DAN waved and motioned the three men over to the table where he and Grace sat.

Wes took in the beautiful dining room of the hotel. Sunlight streamed in through the windows framed in white sills. The ceiling was inlaid with copper, each pane framed by painted wooden beams. Several round tables decked out in white tablecloths were dotted around the room, and the dark oak floors sparkled.

Glancing at his companions, Wes led the way. They took seats at the circular table, and he scanned the room for his parents.

"If you're looking for mom and dad, they already left." Dan took a sip of his orange juice. "Mom apparently woke up with a migraine and decided she'd had enough for one weekend."

Guilt surfacing, Wes considered all that had happened in the last twenty-four hours. "I'm sorry I made your wedding so complicated."

Dan shook his head. "Know what, bro? I'm grateful. You and I are gonna be closer now than we've ever been." He slung an arm around Grace's chair. "And the make-up sex was amazing. Right, babe?"

Grace's cheeks glowed, and she laughed. "Yeah, it was pretty good."

Dan eyed his wife. "Only pretty good?"

Mitch leaned back, flexing his arms and resting his hands on the back of his head with a grin. "We had a *pretty good* night as well."

Cocking an eyebrow, Grace raked her gaze over Clark's date. "I'm sure you did. So, what's the deal with you three? I get the feeling that Clark isn't actually dating you, Mitch."

The smile faded somewhat, but Mitch met Grace's gaze. "What makes you say that?"

"My baby brother tells me everything. Yet, I'd never heard anything about you before this weekend." She shifted her gaze to Wes. "And you know Mitch, too."

Wes exchanged a worried glance with Clark. The heat of his embarrassment surged through his body. *Hell, I'm blushing again.*

Clark cleared his throat, and they all focused on him. "Well, let's just say we all met separately and didn't know it until this weekend."

Pressing forward, Grace's eyes flashed with curiosity. "But *where* did you meet Mitch."

"At a coffee shop," Clark stated carefully. Before she could say anything else, her brother shook his head and crossed his arms. "I think you know enough, and maybe *someday* I'll give you more of the details. But not *this* morning. Suffice it to say, we're all just good friends."

With one last attempt, Grace narrowed her eyes at the

escort. "Mitch?"

He rested his hands in his lap and shrugged. "What the boss there said."

Wes narrowed his gaze, trying to read the expression that flashed briefly across Mitch's face. He seemed disappointed, maybe even sad at Clark's words.

Her eyes lit up with delight. "Boss?"

Dan tapped her shoulder and gave her a squeeze. "Come on, babe. Give it a rest. We've embarrassed them enough."

She zeroed in on her brother. "We'll chat about this later."

"Thanks, Dan." Relief settled over Wes, grateful for the end of the inquisition. He reached for the coffee pot and poured himself a cup.

"No problem, bro." He gave his bride a kiss on the cheek. "But when you finally do tell Grace, I want to be there."

Rolling his eyes, Wes passed the coffee pot to Mitch. "Oh, good grief."

CLARK STEPPED INTO the morning sunshine outside of the hotel, taking in the crisp air and the lazy street. A few people strolled along the sidewalks of downtown Anacortes, but this early on a Sunday morning, few had ventured out.

Leif pushed open the hotel door and nearly bumped into him. "Oh, sorry, Clark. Didn't see you there." He hefted two suitcases. "I have mom's bags. She packs like she's moving or something."

Laughing, Clark nodded. "My mom's like that, too. Nice of you to carry the bags though."

Leif shrugged. "Son-ly duty, right?"

"I hear ya."

"Hey, uh," Leif paused, concern and anxiety playing across his face. "Can I ask you something?"

Fixing his gaze firmly on Leif, Clark nodded. "Sure, cuz. What's up?"

"You brought a guy to the wedding, and no one batted an eye." He fidgeted, his grey gaze fixed on Clark's.

With a chuckle, Clark shook his head. "Almost no one. You missed a bunch of the drama yesterday morning."

"Yeah?" His face deflated. "Were your mom and dad upset you brought a guy?" He breath caught. "Or my mom?"

"What?" Clark jolted, hardly able to envision his parents or his aunt being anything other than supportive. "You're kidding, right? Our family is awesome to me. No, Dan's parents were pretty freaked out that 'the gay' had the nerve to bring a man and try to turn their innocent, straight son."

He screwed up his face. "You mean Grace's husband?"

Another laugh escaped Clark's lips. "No, Wes."

"Oh, right." Leif hesitated a moment. "So, our family was cool with you and Mitch?"

For a big, burly firefighter, Leif's nervous questions and posture reminded Clark of their childhood when his little cousin stood off to the side, afraid of his own shadow.

"Leif, what's going on?" Clark asked, laying a hand on his cousin's shoulder. "Our family is wonderful, and Dan's proving to be surprisingly supportive as well."

Leif's face reddened. He puffed out a breath. "I'm gay."

"Whoa, what?" Clark stared hard at Leif. "No way."

Leif sighed heavily. "I tried to tell you at Christmas Eve dinner, but we never had a minute alone."

"Wow," Clark said with a shake of his head. "My gaydar must be getting rusty. I had no idea."

"It feels good to finally tell someone." He nibbled his bottom lip. "Do you think I should say something to my mom and Duncan?"

"That's totally up to you, Leif. I don't think either of them will have any problem." He set a grin on his face. "Are you dating someone?"

"What? No!" Leif turned a deeper shade of red. "Nobody would want to date me."

With an incredulous laugh, Clark rolled his eyes. "Oh, please. You're twenty-seven, tall, muscular, and a *fireman*, for goodness sake. Every gay man's wet dream." Leif had always been the one to doubt himself, hiding in the shadow of his older brother. Duncan was a great guy, but his outgoing personality had kept his younger brother from blossoming. "Once you get some self-confidence, you'll have plenty of guys chasing you."

"You're the best." Leif stepped forward and wrapped his long arms around Clark.

Clark patted his back. "How about after the dust settles on this weekend, you and I get together for lunch or dinner. I'll give you an idea of what you can expect. There are definitely some dos and don'ts with gay dating."

With a bright smile, Leif released the embrace. "I have Thursday off."

Laughing, Clark nodded. "I'll have your membership card ready."

WITH THEIR BAGS all packed and piled beside the door, Clark, Wes, and Mitch sat around their hotel room.

Clark checked his cell for the time. "It's nearly check-out time." He sighed. "Now that everything is over, I'm a little sad to go back to Seattle." His time with Mitch had come to a close, and they had to get home. If they'd had more time, Clark would've happily repeated the previous evening's fun.

Wes shook his head. "I'm ready to leave this weekend behind. The fallout will be ongoing for me."

Mitch patted his leg. "Do you think your family will make things difficult for you?"

"Hard to say." He lifted his head. "I don't care, though. Only one of my secrets is out of the bag, and that's plenty for one weekend."

Clark laughed. "I'm glad I discovered both of your secrets."

"It would have sucked to be the only one of the wedding party who didn't get laid." His gaze turned fully onto Clark. "Seriously, though. Thank you for helping me come out, and for helping me see that my brother does actually care about me."

Mitch leaned back in his chair, his face painted with a smile. "I think he cares a lot. Just took the shock of almost losing you to shake him out of his stupid behavior."

Butterflies fluttered in Clark's stomach. "So, Wes, um…I never really asked. Are you dating anyone?"

He shook his head. "Nope, but I have my sights set on a really awesome guy."

"Oh, uh, that's cool." Disappointment stung at Clark, and he turned away. *So much for our date.*

"Hey."

Clark turned back to Wes.

"That would be you." A smirk slid across Wes's lips. "Do you think my mother's head would explode if I asked you out on a date?"

Relief morphed into happiness, and Clark held Wes's gaze. "Don't care. I know Grace would be pleased as punch."

"Well, looks like I lost two clients this weekend." Mitch let out an over-exaggerated sigh and waggled his eyebrows.

Clark gave Wes a quick glance and was met with a small nod. "Not necessarily."

Epilogue

"HEY, HONEY, HAVE you seen the box with the frying pan in it?" Clark sorted through the large cardboard box labeled *Clark Kitchen*, not finding what he wanted.

"There's another box under the table," Wes called from somewhere else inside the condo.

Tanner carried another box into the kitchen. "I think this is the last one."

Moving from the stove, Clark took the box from the young man and placed it on the counter. "Thanks." He checked the side of the box. *Kitchen – M.* His face warming, he shot a nervous glance at his sister, who waddled to the table.

She struggled to the floor. "Yup, here it is." She hefted the small box onto the table. "The cast-iron is definitely in here."

"What do you think you're doing, pregnant lady? No lifting the heavy boxes." Stepping across the room, Clark picked up a pair of scissors and cut the tape securing the lid. He parted the cardboard and lifted out three ceramic frying pans and a cast-iron skillet.

She rolled her eyes. "I'm not helpless, Clark," she

muttered.

Tanner chuckled. "I'd better get going. My accounting prof gave us a huge pile of homework this weekend."

Clark lifted the frying pan out of the box. "How's school going?"

"Great," Tanner replied, a happy grin on his face. "I love my classes, and the place I'm renting with a couple guys from the House is working out great."

Clark took a moment to reflect on Tanner's journey. In the three years since he'd been at Firestone House, Tanner had blossomed. The hollow cheeks and too-thin frame of the hungry and homeless teen gave way to a handsome twenty-year-old. He wore his black, straight hair short and spikey, and his features had softened into a healthy dark olive color. Finally graduated from high school, Tanner was in his second year of classes at Seattle Central College, nearly ready to transfer to the University of Washington.

"Glad to hear it." He crossed to Tanner and placed his hand on the young man's shoulder. "I'm really proud of you."

The grin widened. "Thanks. You've been amazing." He stretched out his arms, and Clark gave him a hug. "Oh," Tanner said, breaking away. "I balanced the bank account. There was a weird little error in the books, but I figured it out and fixed it. I left the paperwork on your desk."

"You're going to put me out of a job." Clark chuckled.

"Nah," Tanner replied. "I still don't know how to do all the grant stuff."

"Say goodbye to Wes on your way out, and I'll see you on Monday." He gave Tanner's shoulder one last pat.

Tanner threw a wave and headed out the door. "Will do."

Grace stood next to him. "Great kid. You do wonderful work at that center."

"Kids like him make my job rewarding." He stared after Tanner, smiling when he watched the younger man give Wes a hug.

Returning to the kitchen table, Grace took a chair and eased herself down. "So, you're finally moving in with Wes. What took so long? It's been three years since you met him." She patted her very pregnant tummy. "We're already expecting your second nephew."

Clark shrugged. "Wes has been living at my apartment for the last six months, you know." Stooping down, he pulled open the drawer under the oven and deposited the pans into the empty space. "There's nothing wrong in taking our time to find a place we both liked. Finding something suitable *and* affordable in Seattle isn't easy."

"Are you glad you bought?" She rose and crossed to the box on the counter. Unpacking several spice jars, she lined them up on the granite surface.

"Definitely. House values seem to just keep going up. We got lucky with this place." Staring out the kitchen window at the view of the Olympic Mountains, he marveled at the timing of their purchase. One of Mitch's former clients had needed to sell quickly to close on some business deal in Dubai. The prior owner hadn't really needed the money but wanted to offload the condo. Mitch had arranged a meeting, and the guy had let them have it for a song. He suspected Mitch had done some less-than-conventional types of negotiating to get the price into their range, but their friend didn't kiss and tell.

Grace sniffed at one of the jars. "This one's lost its scent." She held out a mostly empty spice container.

Turning back from the view, he looked at the label. "Oh, that's the marjoram I got a few years ago. I didn't even think to go through the spice cabinet before I packed. You can empty the marjoram into the compost bin, but I'll reuse the glass jar."

She turned and lifted the lid of the ceramic bin sitting on the counter by the stove. "How's Mitch doing? Do you ever see him?"

"Yeah, we see him occasionally." Heat slowly rose into his face. "He's been traveling for business." Another former client had asked Mitch on a round-the-world tour six months ago. He was finally back, but his return had presented a problem for Clark.

"You still never explained what was going on with you three at my wedding." She placed the empty jar in the sink and zeroed her gaze on him.

Rolling his eyes, he turned away and returned to the box full of kitchen implements he'd been searching through earlier. "We've been over this, Grace. He's a friend that both Wes and I knew. We didn't realize we all knew each other until the night before your wedding."

She smirked. "Where you all got *really* well-acquainted."

Wes stepped around the corner and into the kitchen.

"Grace, you're relentless."

Laughing, she opened the cabinet next to the stove. "This one okay for the spices?"

Clark nodded. "Sure."

"Why did Mitch call you boss?" She lined up the glass containers on the shelf.

"Leave it, Grace," Clark huffed. "I've told you all you ever need to know about that night. Be happy everything worked out like it did." He crossed to Wes, who stood silently by, his eyebrows rising and his smile deepening. Wes likely wondered if he'd finally spill the fact he'd hired Mitch to be his date. Clark gave a subtle shake of his head and wrapped an arm around his lover's waist. "Dan found his backbone, and I found the man of my dreams."

"Aw, thanks, honey." Wes gave him a quick kiss on his lips.

The front door of the condo slammed closed. "Hey, boys, I'm home." Mitch's voice called out from the living room.

The warmth drained from Clark's face, and he exchanged a wide-eyed glance with Wes, who'd also lost some color. They both turned to Grace who looked like the cat who'd licked up all the cream.

Mitch stepped into the kitchen. "How're my two lov—oh, uh, hey there, Grace."

"Well, Mitch," she purred. "What a pleasant surprise." Grace swung her piercing gaze at her brother. "And he has his own key, too. Interesting."

With a sigh, Wes pulled Clark across the kitchen and wrapped his other arm around Mitch's waist. "Man, you would have had to tell her eventually. At least she didn't find us all naked like Dan did."

Grace crossed her arms, a smug grin plastered across her face. "I *knew* there was more to the story." She stared them down before continuing, and Clark felt that the odds of three against one were definitely *not* in his favor. "So, Dan and I have a theory about you three."

Clark met Wes's reddening face and Mitch's amused gaze. "Uh oh."

"Here are the pieces of the Clark-Mitch-Wes puzzle we've managed to assemble." The smug lilt to her voice made Clark wince. She always knew how to draw out her torture. "You all knew each other separately, but not together, before the wedding. Clark never said a word to me about Mitch before he showed up at the reception hall."

"But, Grace…" Clark spluttered, but she held up a finger to silence him.

"Wes freaked out when he saw the two of you talking and disappeared, only to reappear with you, Clark, looking much calmer and collected." She leveled her stare at Wes. "I watched you run all the way to the bathroom. What happened there?"

Bright red, Wes gripped Clark tighter. "I wasn't feeling well. Clark sweetly brought me some seltzer water."

She arched an eyebrow. "Interesting that he knew to do it, being all the way across the room huddled with his date." Her gaze settled on Mitch. "And then we have Mister Smooth. All the right words—until he's cornered about seducing my brother-in-law."

Now, it was Mitch's turn to squirm. He reached across Wes's back to clutch Clark's arm.

Though reassuring to have contact with both his lovers, his sister's inquisition had Clark panicked.

"Well, Grace, wouldn't you be—" Mitch tried to speak, but again she held up her finger.

"Shush now, I'm not finished." Her smirk broadened. "Then, after you told Mom he'd agreed to *accompany* you to the wedding, not that you were dating, he called you *boss* at breakfast." She settled her gaze on Clark.

He sucked in a quick breath. "Grace, are you sure you want to go any farther?"

Now, she outright laughed. "Oh, baby brother, of *course* I want to go farther. This is fun."

Clark turned, rested his forehead on Wes's shoulder, and closed his eyes while clutching Mitch's arm tighter. "Tell me when it's over. I can't watch."

Wes patted his side. "Who knew your sister was such a torturess?"

Chuckling, Mitch squeezed Clark's arm again. "She should write fiction with such an overactive imagination."

"Dan and I have discussed this at length. He's just as curious as I am about you boys." She stepped closer to them and pointed to Mitch. "I'm guessing you were a hired date for my brother."

Squeezing his eyes tighter, Clark burned in embarrassment. "Oh my God."

"And Wes engaged your services, too." The triumphant ring in Grace's voice made it all the worse.

Wes sagged. "Shit."

Coming to their defense, Mitch stepped forward. "An interesting theory, Grace. But how do you explain my engineering knowledge when I was speaking to your father?"

Clark opened his eyes, swinging his gaze to his sister to gauge her reaction. "Nice one, Mitch."

He grinned. "Thanks."

"Easy." She held her ground. "You're obviously educated. You told Dad University of Illinois. How did you pay for school?"

"Well, uh…" Mitch began, momentarily losing his smooth demeanor.

Clark cut him off, just wanting the inquisition to be over. "Don't bother. She's rumbled us."

"Ha!" Grace returned to the counter and rested her butt against it. "So, the last question. What is all this?" She waved her hand at the three of them.

Returning to Clark and Wes, Mitch sighed. "This is me leaving the escort business and settling down. I got a job last week at an engineering startup in Pioneer Square."

"And you left such a lucrative business because…?" She trailed off, her gaze firmly fixed on the former escort.

He shrugged. "What can I say? I fell in love with these two. Clark encouraged me to use my degree, so I found something where I can still travel but allows me time to develop a real relationship."

Laughing, she shook her head. "From a parade of losers to a long-term threesome. Good for you, Clark. So, what's your real name, Mitch?"

Wes grinned, a wicked glint resembling Grace's shining in his eyes. "Angus Mitchell Brownlie, poor guy. We call him Mitch."

Mitch's smooth demeanor fell away. "I can't believe you just told her my first name." His eyes narrowed at Wes. "She's not the only tortress."

"I'm glad you're home to stay," Clark replied, drawing Mitch's attention. "You'll get to share in the fun." With a grin, Clark waggled his eyebrows. "Angus."

Rolling his eyes, Mitch turned to Grace. "Please, don't call me Angus," he said, the plea heavy in his voice. "My Scottish parents thought it was a great name, but I prefer Mitch."

A buzzing filled the kitchen, and Grace pulled her phone from her jeans pocket. "Dan's here with Colby."

Grateful for the change of topic, Clark stepped away from Wes and headed for the hallway. "Let's go greet them."

The distraction of his nephew's arrival barely lasted a moment. Grace's smirk returned to her lips. "Sure. He's gonna love hearing what I've uncovered."

Clark swung around. "Look, Grace. Good for you figuring out what our relationship is—but, come on. You're no saint."

Wes and Mitch glanced at each other, and Mitch's eyebrow hitched up. "Care to share?"

"Their names were—"

Her smirk faltered. "No, Clark. You promised never to tell."

Now, it was Clark's turn to smirk. "I'm not sure the word *never* was included in that promise."

She held up her hands. "Okay, okay. Let me tell Dan, but I swear it won't go any farther."

A horn honked twice outside.

Clark crossed his arms. "I get the same deal, or else you can't tell him."

Frowning, she nodded. "Okay." She pointedly stared at Wes. "But there is no way in hell your parents can find out."

Chuckling, Clark returned to Wes's side. "You know there's no fear of that. Though his mom did send us a box of bathroom towels for the condo. After no contact for the last two years, it was weird." He arched an eyebrow at his sister. "One wonders how she found our new address."

A grin returned to Grace's face. "It *might* have come up in conversation when we told her a second grandchild was on the way." She laughed. "But that was before I knew you and Wes now have a third."

The door buzzer sounded, and Clark hurried to the phone.

"What's going on up there?" Dan's voice crackled through the speaker.

"Sorry, we're just finishing up our negotiations." Clark hit the buzzer.

Wes's eyes widened. "You're letting him up here?"

"Like you said, we're not naked." Clark grinned. "Mitch, why don't you answer the door?"

With a chuckle, Mitch left the kitchen to the sound of the doorbell.

Shaking her head, Grace laughed. "Sometimes, you're terrible to my husband."

Scampering feet sounded from the hardwood floors in the hallway.

"Mommy!" A towheaded little boy toddled into the room.

Grace held out her arms and picked up her son, Colby. "Say hi to Uncle Clark and Uncle Wes."

Colby giggled and waved.

Mitch returned to the kitchen followed by a hesitant and somewhat confused Dan.

"Hey, bro. Hey, Clark." Dan stared at his grinning wife. "What's going on, babe?"

She nodded to Mitch. "I believe you've already met our brothers' *other* lover."

Clark snorted at his sister. "Yeah, Grace, that was subtle."

Wes shook his head. "As a brick through the window."

"Not a major surprise, bro." Dan stood next to his wife. "At least, you've made it official. Wait 'til I tell Mom and Dad."

Frowning, Wes crossed his arms. "Grace…"

Grace gave an exaggerated sigh. "In exchange for information, I promised we'd keep this to ourselves." She gave him a quick kiss. "And you owe me a foot rub."

Dan's eyes widened. "What?" He swung to Mitch. "No way!" He furrowed his brow and turned his stare to Wes. "Seriously?"

Feeling the situation was spiraling out of control, Clark glanced at the clock on the wall. "Don't you three need to be somewhere?"

Grace shrugged. "Probably." Seeing his frown, she

giggled. "Yes, we do, but there's only one more thing."

"Isn't there always?" Clark huffed.

She went on, ignoring his rhetorical question. "I'm thinking I've got enough leverage over you three for some free babysitting."

Not letting on that he was excited at the prospect of spending time with his nephew, Clark did his best to maintain his furrowed brow, the muscle in his cheek pulling one side of his mouth downward. "I guess."

Wes jabbed him in the ribs with his elbow. "You're not fooling anyone." He addressed Grace and Dan. "You don't need leverage for that. We'd be thrilled to watch Colby, and the new arrival when he comes along."

"Thanks." Grace kissed her brother. "Say bye-bye, Clark."

Clark replaced his frown with a wide grin and waved at Colby. "Bye-Bye."

Colby mimicked the wave. "Bye-Bye."

A happy warmth spread through Clark. He adored his little nephew. "Let us know when you want us to take Colby."

Dan gave Wes a quick hug. "Love ya, bro." He turned to Clark with another quick embrace. "And you, too, bro."

Hovering by the stove, Mitch waved to Grace and Dan. "Nice to see you both again."

Grace stepped over to him, Colby firmly in her arm. "Say bye-bye to Uncle Mitch."

Colby chewed at his lower lip and shyly raised a hand before quickly turning and burying his face in his mother's shoulder.

Mitch looked over the moon with happiness when Grace gave him a quick hug.

She moved away, and Dan stepped over to him. "Nice to see you, bro." He also gave Mitch a quick hug, and then headed into the hallway.

Clark gave an elated Mitch a thumbs-up, and accompanied his sister and her family to the front door. After Dan took Colby and stepped into the building's hallway, Clark caught her shoulder.

"Seriously, sis. Please don't tell Mom and Dad or your in-laws about me hiring an escort to take to your wedding."

"You're in a three-way relationship, and *that's* what you're concerned about with the in-laws?" She laughed and hugged him again. "Don't worry about it. Neither of us will tell on you." She glanced across the room at Mitch and Wes. "Besides, how lucky are you to have *two* great guys. I'm really happy for you."

"Let's go, Gracie." Dan called from down the hallway.

"Okay, really gotta go. Love you, baby brother." She kissed his cheek.

"Love you, too." Clark shut the door and turned to his lovers. "I'll bet Grace and Dan drop Colby off tomorrow."

Wes nodded. "That's fine. Emily's letting me work from home anyway."

Sitting on the couch in the living room, Clark and Wes faced Mitch who took the easy chair. Several boxes were stacked against one wall still needing to be unpacked, and a few framed paintings were propped against another wall.

Wes leaned back. "Congratulations on the job, Mitch. Are you sad to leave the escorting behind?"

With a shake of his head, Mitch settled into the chair. "Not at all. I'm happy to be here with you both, and Clark was right about the engineering job being much more lucrative. I also don't have to worry about catching anything from my clients."

Clark nodded. "That is a relief." Unlike the other two, he leaned forward on the couch, curiosity niggling at his thoughts. "Since our secrets are getting aired this afternoon, you never did tell us how you got that guy to sell us the condo for such a good price."

With a twinkle in his eyes, Mitch rose from the chair and extended his hand. "Come into the bedroom, and I'll show you."

Did you enjoy *The Wedding Weekend*? If so, look for *Saving Parker*, Book Five of the Rain City Tales coming in August 2018!

ALSO BY BRENT ARCHER

The Golden Scepter Series
The Bastard's Key
Pennington's Conquest
The Hurricane's Triangle

Short Stories
Halfway Out of the Dark
The Christmas Proposal
Summer Stalked

Rain City Tales
The Officer's Siren (Book 1)
Past Secrets Present Danger (Book 2)
I'm Yours (Book 3)
The Wedding Weekend (Book 4)
Saving Parker (Book 5) – Coming August 2018

About the Author

Brent Archer was born in Spokane, Washington, and lived there most of his adolescent life. At 18, he left for Seattle to attend the University of Washington for Electrical Engineering. Quickly, it became apparent that he hated his science classes, and so he switched his major to International Studies with a minor in history. After graduation, he pursued an acting career in musical theater and dance. Once thirty hit, however, he decided to focus on numbers, getting a certificate in accounting, and became the Financial Controller of a non-profit arts and music organization.

Though writing most of his life, he never thought to submit his work for publication. In 2012, he visited his cousin Delilah Devlin in Arkansas and she prodded him to write a story and submit it. So, he did and it sold right away. With the encouragement of Delilah, his other writing cousin Elle James, and his husband, Brent embarked on a writing career. He's loving the journey, finding inspiration and a story everywhere he goes, whether it be the local coffee shop, driving through each of the United States, or riding the train to explore the world.